ONE EYE OPEN

Can a Dolphin Save the World?

Steve Cameron

Augur Press

British Library Cataloguing in Publication Data.
A catalogue record for this book is available from the British Library.

ISBN 978-0-9571380-1-8

First published 2013 by
Augur Press
Delf House
52, Penicuik Road
Roslin
Midlothian EH25 9LH
United Kingdom

Printed by Lightning Source

ONE EYE OPEN

"It is an important and popular fact that things are not always what they seem.

"For instance, on the planet Earth, man has always assumed that he was much more intelligent than dolphins because he had achieved so much – the wheel, New York, wars and so on – whilst all the dolphins had ever done was muck about in the water having a good time.

"But conversely, the dolphins had always believed that they were far more intelligent than man – for precisely the same reasons."

– Douglas Adams
'The Hitchhikers' Guide to the Galaxy'

DEDICATION

For my sister Kristi, who has battled illness for so horribly long and deserves some joy.

And to Mary Imms, who would not quit pushing, even when the goal seemed out of our reach.

ACKNOWLEDGEMENTS

No matter if this book sells a dozen copies or a million, for me it's already a winner. It was originally released in the United States in 2007 under a different title: 'The Chanonry Encounter.'

Mirabelle Maslin of Augur Press in Edinburgh, bless her, saw the potential and also the problems with that first book, and along with my longtime friend and colleague – Sally Masterson of Masterson Media – Mirabelle rescued the entire project.

But for now, allow me to revisit the start of it all.

When I started researching the amazing dolphins of the Moray Firth ten years ago, the work began online. I was hoping to discover where in northern Scotland people could have the closest possible contact with dolphins while remaining on dry land.

Hopping from one link to another, I accidentally made contact with a terrific photographer, Lyn MacDonald, who lived in the area and had been shooting pictures of the local dolphins for years. She was glad to answer my endless questions, and ultimately we chatted over the internet about the book project, about life in general, about lots of things. Ultimately, Lyn became my friend for life.

Several people encouraged me in those days, even when things seemed difficult – and at times, they were, because the problems with my arms and shoulders (as described in the book) were very real indeed.

Good friends fought their way through every draft, suggesting changes and catching mistakes. Both Lyn and my sister, Kris, pointed out that in the original manuscript,

Jill Gabriel seemed 'too perfect'. So Jill acquired a few little quirks, here and there, and I think that my fictional partner in this adventure actually does seem more 'real' after several drafts and changes.

Any author who completes a book will tell you that it could not have happened without the help of countless pals, sources or partners. And it's so true in this case that I hardly know where to begin.

Let's start with the people who helped to turn the first manuscript into the published novel 'The Chanonry Encounter.' You wouldn't be reading this without them. They weren't just cheerleaders. They put a lot into the project.

I touch my hat to my colleagues at the Merced Sun-Star, a newspaper in California, where I was working when that first book actually was completed. My boss and friend, Joe Kieta (now editor of the Modesto Bee), gave me the time and encouragement to write.

The fantastic cover photograph of 'The Chanonry Encounter' was taken by Lyn MacDonald. She also kindly made available several other dramatic photos for our current venture.

Needless to say, any errors in the books are my responsibility alone, but there would be an awful lot more without the relentless proof-reading of Mike Patrick, a crackerjack editor and a friend of many years.

And then, along came Mirabelle and her staff at Augur Press, who converted my new version of the manuscript to 'UK English' – and also edited 'One Eye Open.'

I am incredibly grateful to all those people.

I owe more than thanks to Marc Garcia, Tim Leach, Mary and Marge Imms – along with my sister and her husband, Frank – for investing in this project at the very beginning. With a lot of travelling around two continents, it became fairly expensive.

Thank you all.

It stuns me still to think of all the help and ideas that came from this group, from suggestions on the manuscript all the way to marketing ideas.

There was a time when the writing of 'The Chanonry Encounter' was slightly stalled as I wrestled with the puzzling question of how dolphins could be so incredibly intelligent, and possess so many physical capabilities, but yet many of them could be caught in nets or even killed by sharks. I was stymied by that apparent paradox, especially considering the dolphins' mysterious stunning ability, which they use only to kill or paralyse fish for food.

During a wonderful, all-night conversation with Tim Leach in a Las Vegas hotel room, he put into words something which I believed but couldn't quite describe.

'After thirty million years of evolution,' Tim said, 'it stands to reason that dolphins would have developed a "higher morality" than anything grasped by man. Dolphins would simply and naturally understand the need for balance in the world, rather than having any desire to dominate it.'

With that moment of enlightenment, courtesy of Tim, the writing – and the dolphins' rationale for what they do in this novel – became so much easier to piece together.

I'm always afraid of leaving out some important people, but I'll do my best. I owe incredible gratitude to Kris Simpson and Robin Petch of the SeaWatch Foundation. Robin and Kris have spent countless hours in the water swimming freely with dolphins. Talking to Robin and Kris convinced me even more just how close we might be to easy and genuine mutual communication with these fantastic creatures.

Finally, as always, I need to thank my own personal support group – family, friends, co-workers and so forth.

These are the people who inspire you to dream big, and who enable you to try things you might otherwise let slide.

Lyn's terrific daughters, Kerri and Daisy, had a significant part to play -- and Myrtle Beach never will be the same without them.

Some of my longtime pals have been around for the entire journey – all the way through the 14 books that I have written to date. Thanks again to folks like Jeff Flanagan, John Genzale, Bob Casey, Tim Keithley, Tommy Stewart, Beckie Rathke and so many others.

And then there are my 'lads' from the Arsenal Scotland Supporters Club, the boys who keep me chuckling every day and make all my time in Britain a treasure – Fraz Mackenzie, Martin O'Donnell, Euan Esselmont, Mike Buchanan, Marek Streicher (thanks for the Slovakia World Cup shirt...), the infamous Jabs and all the rest. Yes, I'll continue to be the funny sounding Yank on a lot more train and coach trips, fellow Gooners.

Now we move to the second phase of the journey. This novel probably would have died completely after our failed first attempt at marketing it ourselves in the United States, if it weren't for the fact that Mirabelle was there to see some value in the story -- and suggest that it could be released in the United Kingdom.

But it was the very special Melissa Gwin who kept the fire burning during my days of doubt. Without her help and support through the times when all seemed hopeless, we wouldn't be here. Thank you with all my heart – and that goes for you, too, Matthew.

Here's a nod once again to Lyn MacDonald for the photographs that appear on the web site dedicated to 'One Eye Open.' And thanks also to Ismailova Gruppa, who designed the book cover.

Everyone mentioned, and dozens more, all helped to make this book a reality. To all of you, I apologise for dawdling so long.

There is a scene in a movie called 'Elizabethtown,' in which the lead character, played by Orlando Bloom, is just about to give up on life when his father unexpectedly dies of a heart attack. At the urging of his upbeat and charming love interest (Kirsten Dunst), the young man agrees to take a cross-country road trip after the funeral – carrying along his father's ashes in an urn which he straps carefully into the passenger seat of his car.

The trip opens the man's eyes to a life and a family that he had let slide away, and at one point while driving across the open roads of America, he says to his deceased father: 'We should have taken this trip years ago.'

Sometimes I feel that way about this book. It's been there, in my head and in my heart without a final product, but...

At last I've listened to all your pep talks, Mimsy! We're taking the trip now, and it feels just great.

STEVE CAMERON

Chapter 1

Fortrose, Scotland

September

I've arrived. I'm on time. I'm cold.

This is Chanonry Point – in northern Scotland. It's a spit of land poking out into the Moray Firth from the southern side of the Black Isle, which is neither black nor an isle. Local historians have advanced no fewer than half a dozen theories about why this area would be called black – from a long association with witches and mysticism and the 'black arts', to the idea that its covering of trees made it look almost black. As for the isle part, no one seems to have any idea.

Until now, the only truly historic event at Chanonry Point occurred in 1660, when a famous local seer called Coinneach Odhar paid the price for being too honest. Odhar, who allegedly foretold dozens of amazing events, was asked by the Countess of Seaforth why her husband was so late returning from an overseas trip. The golden rule of seers – a rule practised even now by consultants wearing Gucci loafers – is to anticipate what the client really wants to hear, and steer the conversation in that direction.

Apparently this mystic was not quite so savvy. Odhar

barged right ahead and broke the news to Lady Seaforth that her Lord was dallying in Paris – with a woman more attractive than the Lady herself.

By all accounts, Odhar was surely able to see into the future. He spoke of the Caledonian canals linking lochs to the sea, and even a bridge that would span the Beauly Firth from Inverness, at a time when such things seemed preposterous. Yet he obviously didn't know much about women.

Lady Seaforth didn't take to his 'vision' kindly. She promptly had Odhar arrested, tried and convicted of witchcraft – all in less than an hour. The seer was then dragged out to Chanonry Point, and was tossed into a barrel of boiling tar.

Not much of note has happened at Chanonry Point since the seer's execution.

In 1846, a lighthouse was built at the tip of the ness, and plenty of sailors over the years must have agreed that it had been a very good idea. And by the way, in case you're not Scottish, ness means a headland or a peninsula. Although it is less than a mile across the firth to Fort George, foul weather can whip in frequently, and with little warning, from the open sea towards Inverness.

There is a caravan park and a little house out near the Point these days, and most of the ness is covered by the Fortrose and Rosemarkie Golf Course. And that's about it, or *was* it, until now.

Among the thoughts that crossed my mind, as I stood, shivering, on the tip of Chanonry Point, was that one of two things had to happen. Either sometime soon I might be having a conversation that would make Odhar's plunge into the tar little more than a footnote in the history of this place, or I was freezing in a September gale for nothing, and might have to pretend that I had never even been here.

So, I wrapped up as well as one can in a windbreaker,

and wondered again: Why *was* I here?

A woman was the cause of it. Actually, it was one very grown-up woman and an 11-year-old girl. No, that's not entirely true. I'd done a little research, talked to a marine biologist, and decided that undertaking an apparently nutty jaunt from Arizona to Houston, to south Florida, to Scotland, to London, and now back to a lonely beach near the Arctic Circle truly was worth the effort.

Could any serious journalist ignore what I'd heard? No, not a chance.

Standing there as dusk fell, and lights twinkled in Inverness – just a few miles to the southeast – and on the Kessock Bridge, the structure Coinneach Odhar had seen in his dreams, I ran it all through my mind one more time.

I thought again of the woman who had got me started – Jill Gabriel. This source of inspiration was a former journalist who had taken a bullet just above her ear while covering the war in Bosnia. Her role during that conflict had been to stand resolutely in front of a camera and deliver terse bulletins back to the BBC in Britain, while bullets pinged off houses and cars around her. She only survived her thirty-third day of reporting on the siege of Sarajevo because one of the partisan fighters, who was crouching in a half-demolished warehouse, saw her doing the daily update and shouted 'Nice ass!' in broken English while he was reloading his AK-47.

The comment about her backside had caused her to turn and look towards the source of the compliment, which meant that a wild shot delivered by a Serbian sniper up the street simply grazed her scalp, instead of splitting her head open, like a melon dropped from the Eiffel Tower. She still saves the front page of a London newspaper which ran this giant headline: 'Lovely Arse Saves TV Babe!' The medical verdict seemed pretty straightforward – several stitches, hairline fracture, but no brain damage.

As the temperature dropped another couple of notches at Chanonry Point, I thought about how she had helped to deliver me here.

But never mind the goose bumps or anything else. The simple truth is that I came out here of my own free will. No, it was more than that. I *wanted* to be at this place, and on this particular day. Crazy idea or not, it was my call. I could blame Jill until morning, but I'd be kidding myself.

She had steered me in this direction, and the little girl had given me a final push – simply because she'd seen and heard things that no self-respecting reporter could ignore. At least the youngster insisted she had, and coming to Chanonry Point was the only way I could find out for myself.

I'd sorted it out as best I could the previous night on a train north from London. I've travelled on the sleeper from Euston up to Inverness several times, so I'm quite familiar with the journey. In fact, I'm a bit of a train buff, and it's one of my favourite trips.

With departure at ten past nine in the evening, you head straight to your private compartment, dump the luggage, and go to join the crowd in the lounge car. Wacky accents, hilarious stories, cold drinks all around, lights of north-central England whizzing by the windows for an hour or two, and then to bed, tucked into a cosy wee den.

The trip takes all night, and you wake up to see the proof that you're a long way past the border into Scotland, because all the little stations along the way have signboards written both in English and in Gaelic.

A porter, who's almost always named Angus, taps on your door at dawn, and brings tea and a roll with a copy of the Glasgow Herald. Fluff up the pillow, sip the brew, and let your soothed mind drift gently into the Highlands. It's normally a grand and peaceful ride, but last night I barely slept at all. I think I was just dozing off when it occurred to me that I'd never attempted anything like this. Not even close... and journalists find themselves in a lot of crazy spots.

Yet now, as the sky kept getting darker, and the wind picked up another few miles per hour at Chanonry Point, I replayed all those thoughts and doubts – from the hurried flight to Britain, to my meeting with a brilliant marine expert from the Global Dolphin Society, and to ridiculously fuzzy plans concerning just what might happen if this rendezvous went as planned.

Each time I went over the whole thing I simply stopped right there, because the possible reality was quite beyond me. In any case, there seemed a pretty good chance that whatever came of this would be out of my hands.

Meanwhile, it continued getting colder.

Then, gradually, I saw a shadow slowly appear out of the mist. The shadow turned into a man – a fellow in a long raincoat, with a pair of binoculars draped round his neck. Now, where had this character come from – and what was he doing out in the chilly nowhere of Chanonry Point?

'Cheers,' he said. 'See anythin'?'

'No,' I replied, a little bit reluctantly. Could he conceivably have a clue about my own plans?

'Watchin' for birds m'self,' he explained. 'Been at it forty years. Tough to see much now, though.'

All I could do was nod in agreement.

'Whatcha doin' yerself?' he asked. 'Watchin' the tide?'

I had a brief inclination to laugh out loud. What *was* I doing on this icicle of land that poked out into the Moray Firth?

'It's a crazy story,' I answered. 'You wouldn't believe it.'

'Oh, aye,' was his response. 'Crazy to be out in any case. Prob'ly time for a dram and a fire.'

With that, the birdman disappeared back into the gloom along Ness Road, the direction from which he had come.

Alone once more, I walked over to the stone memorial which commemorates the death of Coinneach Odhar. I couldn't read the inscription in the fading light, but I already knew it by heart.

'Coinneach,' I murmured, 'what do you think?'

There was no answer, of course.

So what was I waiting for? Would it be a splash, or a screech, from somewhere in the eddies that swirl around and whip up the water between the Point and Fort George? Quite frankly, I didn't know. There isn't much precedent for this sort of thing. All I could do was wait, and repeat the bare-bones instructions that I'd been given:

Full moon in September, at high tide. Wait on the north side. A dolphin will come to you. His name is Spike. What he wants is very, very important.

Yes, that last part I could work out for myself. If a dolphin is somehow going to communicate directly with a human being after thirty million years of the species clearing its collective throat...

Well, he probably wasn't going to ask for help doing the *Times* crossword puzzle.

Chapter 2

London

Five years earlier

I had an overwhelming reason to avoid telling that bird-watcher at Chanonry Point my reason for standing around in such a cold, uninviting place. And to be honest, I also didn't want to sound completely off my head.

Let me provide a bit of background. My part in this odyssey began with a wayward whale that became involved in a significant event a few hundred miles away from Chanonry. When I first read about the whale, I didn't have the faintest idea that this story might turn my world upside down.

In the last week of January 2006, an eighteen-foot northern bottlenose whale became disoriented, left its normal feeding grounds in the Atlantic Ocean, and swam up the River Thames to London. For three days, residents of the British capital flocked to bridges and other viewing spots to see the great mammal.

Maritime experts immediately warned that the whale – at one point historically photographed just a few metres from the Houses of Parliament – almost certainly was seriously ill or injured.

Eventually, a group called the British Divers Marine

Life Rescue attempted to transport the whale back out to the open sea. The creature had beached itself several times in apparent confusion, so it was lifted out of the water at Battersea Park. The plan was to transfer the whale to a large vessel, and then take it out into the English Channel and hope that it would regain both its health and its bearings.

Vets on board the rescue vessel were pessimistic about the chances of the whale surviving, because its respiratory rate was far too high. An emergency decision was taken to put the whale back into shallower water at a place called Shivering Sands, off the north Kent coast, but by then it was beginning to suffer convulsions.

The whale died around seven o'clock on a Friday night, and it seemed that the whole nation mourned.

There was some irony in that, since the British whaling industry had enthusiastically slaughtered thousands of the mammals between 1850 and 1973. After that, international agreements had made all whale hunting illegal. The visit of this northern bottlenose to London in 2006 touched hearts everywhere. Thousands of witnesses had lined the riverbank when the whale appeared, and millions more followed the saga on television.

Dr Paul Jepsen, a vet from the Zoological Society of London, was on the rescue barge when the whale died, and he told the Guardian newspaper: 'The odds were slim that we could successfully rescue this whale. We were very worried about its condition. Unfortunately, it did deteriorate very quickly. A decision was made to euthanise the animal because of its suffering, but before this could take place, the whale sadly died.'

Dr Jepsen was heartened by the public response to the whale's plight, and he went on to say: 'Many children may remember seeing this bottlenose whale in London, and in the future I hope they may become mammal enthusiasts and conservationists.'

Emma Sterling of the International Fund for Animals sounded even more hopeful, and talked about working to save the species throughout the world.

'Tragically, it's too late for this whale, but Japanese vessels are currently pursuing more than a thousand whales in the southern oceans under the pretext of scientific research,' she said. 'Whales around the world face several threats from whaling by Japan, Norway and Iceland, along with pollution and habitat destruction, and increased noise in the ocean. We hope the whale which visited the UK Houses of Parliament can act as an ambassador for all whales, and that its death won't be in vain.'

The pleas from Sterling and from others did not go unheeded. About a month after the whale had visited London, the British government's Committee on Marine Science and Technology came to the conclusion that sea mammals are being affected dramatically by many unnatural sounds, including sonar, oil exploration and shipping.

This committee recommended that intense research into ocean sounds be commissioned, and even suggested that such mammals might be deliberately exposed to noise as part of an effort to research how long-term difficulties might be prevented.

'There are many sources of sound in the sea, including seismic surveys for hydrocarbon prospecting, shipping, offshore wind farms, military sonars and scientific research,' reported Peter Liss, a professor from the University of East Anglia who chaired the committee. 'We therefore decided that the study must consider all these sectors, and one of our conclusions is the need for better regulation, underpinned by more research.'

The committee noted that there had been numerous

unexplained beachings and strandings of whales and dolphins around the world, and pointed out that because of some of these, legal cases had been brought against the United States Navy and military arms of other countries.

According to a report carried by the BBC, the suggestion of the committee that 'controlled exposure experiments' be conducted – documenting the reaction of whales, dolphins and other sea animals to sounds mimicking the noise of sonar, oil drilling and other activities – was certain to be controversial. The committee conceded that its ideas had aroused 'ethical, political and practical issues' with regard to testing through simulated noise experiments, but it concluded that the benefits would outweigh any potential risks, if the research were regulated properly.

I remember reading and re-reading that BBC story on the committee's concerns and recommendations, and wondering what would come of it all.

Coincidentally, during the same week that the BBC report was released and carried on the news agency's online site, I was thousands of miles away – also thinking of marine mammals, although for an entirely different reason. I was suffering pain in both shoulders from years of typing – as a newspaper and magazine journalist – and was in the process of phoning several friends who claimed they'd found relief from various aches and pains by swimming with dolphins.

Yes… dolphins.

The results of those encounters sounded encouraging, and I decided that if the discomfort in my shoulders worsened, and standard medical remedies continued to be useless, perhaps I'd visit a dolphin park. There are regular sessions at these places – opportunities for anyone at all to hop into a pool with several dolphins. This is mostly for the experience of being close beside such magnificent creatures, but it's also because people with complaints ranging from depression to gout have insisted that interacting with the huge, friendly mammals had somehow lessened their symptoms, or made them disappear completely.

At that time, however, I had no reason to make the slightest connection between my own joint aches and any fallout from that whale's sad swim through the centre of London.

Just a few years later, that situation changed – and quite dramatically.

Chapter 3

Arizona, Texas and Florida

August

I can't imagine a reason, other than business, that would lure me to Houston. And even business – in this case, pursuit of a magazine story that gave me a few journalistic tingles – cannot make Houston attractive, interesting, or cooler.

A city with such staggering humidity that it builds an entire system of tunnels under its sprawling downtown, simply so that pedestrians don't have to step outside into a mind-numbing steam bath, is fighting an uphill battle. So yes, you can assume I had a pretty good reason when I found myself on a flight to Houston in the middle of summer.

I am a freelance author and journalist. I have several books and countless magazine articles on my CV, so I know the two basic rules of the business. The first is that you should live somewhere nice – and northern Arizona's pine forests, combined with an oddball collection of locals in the smallish university city of Flagstaff, provide an unusual kind of charm. It's a lovely, wacky sort of place, and an excellent venue for a writer to work – or just hang around when there's nothing on his plate.

The second rule is that you venture out only when paid decently for something you find interesting.

One afternoon I got a phone call...

It was the editor of Southwest Life magazine, a fellow called Bo Tremaine. In just a few minutes, he'd managed to cover the issue of compensation and add just enough curiosity to get me interested. The speed of all this was a very good thing, as well, because Bo is pretty much deaf from Gulf War artillery shells, and so he tends to shout non-stop.

Absorbing Bo's verbal assault for any length of time requires industrial-strength headache medicine, so it's always best to bring him right to the point and make a decision quickly – even rashly, if necessary. Blessedly, this particular phone call was completed in something near record time.

Bo blasted out his greeting: 'Hey, remember Reies Tijerina?'

He never bothers to say who's ringing. Bo must assume that hardly anyone else would begin shouting for no particular reason. The trick with Bo – and it's not as easy as you think – is to holler back at the proper pitch, while reminding yourself that only one of you is hard of hearing. You want him to get the message without screaming yourself hoarse.

'Let me guess,' I replied, stalling because Tijerina's name rang a bell somewhere off in the distance, but I couldn't quite tune into it. 'A Colombian soccer player?'

'You're fooling with me,' Bo grumbled. 'C'mon, think of New Mexico.'

Ah, yes, I did know Reies Lopez Tijerina, and had written about him years before in some historical retrospective about the plight of Mexican-American landowners – people who had been run off their own soil by the US government. Tijerina was part of a crowd that

13

sought to overturn the 1848 Treaty of Guadalupe Hidalgo, which basically swallowed huge gulps of land from Mexico in return for, well... nothing. This was American foreign policy in its chest-pounding glory.

Tijerina was a 1960s firebrand who organised a gang called the Alianza, and one sleepy summer day in '67, Reies and a few of his gang shot up the courthouse in Tierra Amarilla, New Mexico, up near the Colorado border. They were planning to arrest the sheriff of Rio Arriba county – a curious choice, since the county itself is a sad patch of land with fewer than 40,000 people scattered across endless miles of scruffy hills and dusty arroyos.

The raid was a mess. It turned out that the sheriff was out of town. Two people were shot, and the Alianza ended up fleeing in all directions. Tijerina became the patron saint of what later was known as the *chicano* movement. He was arrested for various bits of civil mischief in '69 and did some prison time. End of story. Well, more or less...

As far as I knew, there were still some bullet holes in the old Rio Arriba courthouse, but nothing else had happened in the place over the past four and a half decades that possibly would rate more than a couple of paragraphs.

'Bo, why in the world would you ask me about Tijerina?' I asked.

'Well, is the guy still alive?' he demanded in deafening tones.

'No clue.'

'Hey, maybe he is,' Bo shouted, 'because over the last two weeks, there have been three fires set in Houston. Yes, definitely arson, and all in buildings owned by Anglos who sell stuff to Hispanics. And each time, the cops have found a bunch of green chile peppers tied to notes that say: "Sons of Reies." '

Damn, I thought.

Aloud, I said, 'You know that green chiles don't grow in Houston.'

The voice on the line rose to an ear-splitting level. 'Man, now I remember why I phoned. I was looking for a writer who dabbles in horticulture.'

'No need to be snide, Bo. Shall I guess? You want me to go and see what's up in Houston, and maybe find out if Tijerina is alive while I'm at it? If he is, he's got to be about ninety years old.'

My response was greeted with a bark so loud that I almost dropped the phone.

'He'll be eighty-six on September 21,' Bo screeched. 'And I'll bet you didn't know he was born in Texas, either. Came from a family of sharecroppers, right there in Texas – a place called Falls City.'

Bo clearly thought he smelled the scent of a story – one of the rougher kind that Southwest Life likes to trumpet as a balance to its design-your-own-swimming-pool features. He wanted me to go and sniff it out – in Houston, in the sweatbox of summer.

'Usual fee up front and all that,' he hollered. 'There's a ticket in your name at the Flagstaff airport. Should be a short layover in Phoenix. You'll be in Houston tomorrow afternoon. Call me when you find out who's having a barbecue with those green peppers.'

'Ticket waiting?' I said. 'You're kind of taking me for granted, Bo.'

'You doin' anything better?'

I was trying to think of a clever reply when I realised that he'd hung up. His voice still seemed to be echoing through the house – which was not surprising, since two people had been yelling throughout an entire phone conversation.

And so I was bound for the horrible humidity of

Houston to look for the ghost of Reies Tijerina. To be honest, this odd mission sounded a bit interesting, perhaps with a hint of intrigue – racial tension, spiced by arson and green peppers.

So, of course, I responded as directed. I trooped off, picked up the tickets, packed a good brand of extra-strength deodorant and flew to Houston. And as a matter of fact, I jumped right into the story – which unfortunately was a dud.

It turned out that the search for the scorched peppers, and maybe a tale of serious civil unrest, came apart in less than a week of talking to bored cops and faintly surly Hispanic activists. The arsonists, one of whom had seen a video about Tijerina and had decided to borrow his name, were caught with incredibly dull efficiency.

Apparently, the bad guys ran out of green peppers – which really don't grow properly anywhere but Hatch, New Mexico – and tried to order another batch... on the internet. A cop with a computer ran down the Houston address in about five minutes, the would-be terrorists were discovered in a two-bedroom house packed with jet fuel, and everyone surrendered peacefully.

The only casualty was the woman next door, who fainted at the thought of all those explosives just a few feet away, especially since her husband smoked Cohiba cigars at the rate of maybe a dozen a day.

So much for a flaming urban uprising in Houston. Bo had me write a few hundred words for a little notebook feature which he called 'Southwest Sunsets', and I banked a nice fee for very little work – unless you count surviving Houston as gainful employment. The whole visit to Texas should have been totally unimportant, but events afterwards made it one of the most crucial journeys I'd ever taken.

Why? Well, that's a lot better a story than the green

peppers. And it began on the plane en route to Houston – before I'd even had a chance to start hunting down those supposed 'terrorists'.

You see, on the flight from Phoenix to Houston, I met a woman called Samantha Simon. In a crazy, roundabout way, she helped convince me to start a journey that bounced off both sides of the Atlantic Ocean and left me wondering about some amazing things. It also led me to guess whether my sanity or my credit card limit would give out first.

And by the way, it was quite by accident that I ended up sitting next to Samantha, who was intensely interested in two things – ordering more of those little plastic glasses filled with rum and Coke, and grilling me about what I did for a living. She noticed my work bag, in which I was probably fishing for a Snickers bar or something equally unimportant, and asked me point-blank if I was a lawyer.

'Hell, no,' I replied, slightly indignant because, like most other Americans, I've paid so many attorneys for needless work that it's a miracle I'm not living in a cardboard box under a bridge somewhere. 'Actually I'm a journalist.'

At this point, Ms Simon nearly jumped out of her seat.

'Then tell me this,' she asked, sloshing a little rum on my new Nikes. 'Have you ever written anything about the Mafia?'

'Well, yes, a long time ago.'

'Okay,' she said. 'What do you know about the murder of Jimmy Hoffa?'

For a second or two, I had no idea what she was talking about, but finally I guessed that she must have some connection to people involved with the Teamsters Union, a powerful and often thuggish organisation that, for years, had turned a labour organisation into what law enforcement officials insisted was a crudely illegal profit centre. But like the tale of Tijerina and his crusade against the government, the Teamsters' heyday had come and gone decades ago.

There was a fascinating and long-standing mystery about what had happened to Hoffa, the Teamsters' boss, who survived a prison sentence, only to disappear sometime later, due to what everyone assumed was foul play. Hoffa had hoped to take back control of the massive union and all its funds, but he went to a lunch meeting in suburban Detroit one afternoon and was never seen again.

Books and TV specials have examined the Hoffa disappearance for years. Assorted gangsters and oddballs, including a convicted Mafia hit man already in prison for life, came forward to claim that they had been present for the abduction and murder of the union boss. It was all nonsense. Every possible connection to the Hoffa affair has been discussed and investigated. Hoffa's body never has been found, no one's been arrested, and every rumour has long since been exhausted.

Sam explained that she was from Detroit – Teamster country because it's the centre of the American auto industry – and that she was living in the Houston area only because her husband was a scientist, and apparently he was trying to unravel the mystery of human genetics for a company that hoped to reap billions from it.

What she actually said was: 'Jim works with mice.'

As the flight droned on, and Samantha made a serious dent in the airline's rum supply, I discovered again what fun it can be to hear outlandish stories from someone who apparently had some passing family connection to assorted bad guys. Where else would things like this come up out of nowhere, except on an airplane ride?

Sam wanted to know if I had ever thought of writing a book about people who had populated the fringes of organised crime.

'Nope,' I replied. 'I've never thought of it.'

'Well, that's crazy,' she said. 'You've got to do it. Absolutely. You owe it to me – I mean, people like me. I want to hear everything. And I'll bet a lot of readers would love to know all these tales. I met someone a few years ago who mailed the head from a cadaver to a researcher looking into the Teamsters Union money dealings. Or at least, that's what he said.'

She paused only for a moment, and then rambled on. 'Look, my mom was really sick most of the time I was growing up, and she died when I was sixteen, so basically I was raised by my dad and my uncle. And they're both, well, guys who were "connected". You know that phrase, right? They're twins, and they're seventy-nine years old now. And, listen, they're going to be together for a visit next month at my father's place in Florida, on Marco Island. You should go down there.'

Me? In Florida? Yes, I realised that we were talking about another really hot place at the wrong time of year. Florida is prettier than Houston, and there are great beaches, but what about the hurricane season?

There was also the issue of whether or not I wanted to meet a couple of men who might have blown up buildings, or heaven knows what else. Not to mention that they surely had plenty of reasons they might not want to spend any quality time with a guy taking notes.

Samantha chattered along. 'Hey, these guys owned sports bars during the 1960s and '70s. They weren't really the violent types, but they knew everybody – you know, guys who might have done all sorts of things. John Vascuso's my dad, and Tommy's his brother. They've got tons of stories from all sorts of celebrities and gangland groupies, and who knows everyone they've hung out with through the years? If you sat down with them for a couple of days, it would be the greatest show on Earth. And I'll bet you'd want to write a book or a magazine story or something about it all. It would be a great. I don't care what you've got going, or what else you're supposed to do. You have to get to Florida next month to sit around with these two old, um…'

'Mobster wannabes?' I suggested.

'Well, not exactly,' Sam replied. 'They weren't really killers or anything. They just knew some crazy guys, and they've got unbelievable stories to tell. It was so long ago that it would all be only rumours by now. But it's the exciting kind of stuff that the public loves. You see mob movies and documentaries all the time, even now.'

This was crazy talk, rum talk, but for a while I forgot about Houston and the green pepper arsons, because the mention of Florida brought another issue to mind. I thought about that non-stop ache in my arms and shoulders. Now, just imagine a writer spending hours at a computer with shooting pains in his shoulders. I'd tried exercises and muscle relaxants for years with no effect at all, and to be perfectly honest, I was on the verge of phoning a guy I knew who'd suffered ripping pains in both wrists from years at a keyboard, and then not long ago had been cured – by dolphins.

Yes, I mean that. It's true. He visited one of those parks where you spend an hour or so in a pool with a few dolphins. What he told me sounded almost like voodoo. He swore that he felt tingling sensations near his hands when the dolphins swam near him, and when he climbed out of the water, the pain had gone.

Frankly, I believed it could be true. I'd read enough books, and heard enough anecdotes about dolphins, to believe that these amazing mammals really do have some ability to cure various types of human ailments. My friend called it the 'ultra ultra-sound' treatment.

There are plenty of swim-with-dolphins parks open to the public, and most of them are in Florida. I couldn't help thinking about what joy it would be to sit down to work again someday without feeling that awful throbbing in my arms.

I've never really been a supporter of keeping dolphins captive as entertainment, but, being honest here, I'd never objected strongly enough to be called an activist.

How could I know at that moment that my opinions about dolphins might change dramatically, and fairly quickly?

'Let me think about this visit and then call you,' I suggested to Sam, unconsciously massaging my shoulders. 'Right now I've got to find out if an old anarchist is trying to burn down Houston with green peppers.'

'What?' said Sam. 'You can make a fire out of peppers? That's nuts.'

'It's probably all just nonsense,' I admitted, without mentioning that the idea of tacking on a trip to Florida for a dolphin miracle cure was probably just as odd.

Samantha and I parted ways at the airport in Houston, but the conversation stuck in my mind. And a card with several phone numbers she'd handed me was jammed safely in my shirt pocket.

So after that little dance with the Tijerina imposters turned out to be no more than a minor annoyance – and certainly not a major magazine story – I had some extra time on my hands.

My shoulders were still sore. I wondered about my own judgment for a bit, but in the end I phoned Samantha. I told her that I was willing to listen to her family's tales, and in practically no time at all, she had convinced me to go and listen to stories on the beach at Marco Island. Of course, I was also thinking that I might search for one of those dolphin parks, but I didn't mention that.

Almost exactly a week after Sam had first quizzed me on the plane about old mob guys and all the rest of it, I found myself at John Vascuso's house – swapping stories with two guys who loved to talk about gambling, nasty men in pinstripe suits and even the fate of the infamous Jimmy Hoffa.

They swore they knew how that whole vanishing act had actually occurred, but I tuned it out. Too much silliness had been written already, and let's face it, these two characters didn't have any better guesses than anyone else.

I really didn't believe that John and Tommy might jump-start a book or even a magazine piece.

So why am I recounting this rather odd trip to Florida? Because of the connection to those nearby dolphins, of course.

Within an hour of my arrival at Marco, Sam had dragged me down to the beach, where the whole family had gathered to watch the sunset. I'd shaken hands with John – whom his oldest pals called 'Johnny Biscuit' – and his brother Tommy. All this conversation was useless to me as an author. Still, it was a bit of fun.

I also met Jim the Mouse Scientist, who turned out to be a perfectly normal fellow. And as I chatted with this man, who worked with thousands of mice in his research, my mind kept returning to thoughts of dolphins with their mysterious abilities. I should have known that my life was going take a wild new turn, and that this was just the first tiny hint.

Looking back, it was all so obvious.

On the flight to Florida, I found that someone had left a printout of *Science Daily*, an online magazine for physicists, molecular biologists and that sort of clientele. I was about to toss it away when I noticed some previous traveller had marked a story about dolphins. Yes, here were dolphins – again. The headline read: 'Dolphins Use Diplomacy in Their Communication, Biologists Find.' Naturally, I'd felt compelled to read it.

'A Spanish researcher and a Paraguayan scientist have presented the most complete and detailed European study into the repertoire of sounds used by bottlenose dolphins (Tursiops truncatus) to communicate. The study reveals the complexity and our lack of understanding about the communication of these marine mammals.

'Until now, the scientific community had thought whistles were the main sounds made by these mammals, and were unaware of the importance and use of burst-pulsed sounds. Researchers from the Bottlenose Dolphin Research Institute, based in Sardinia (Italy), have now shown that these sounds are vital to the animals' social life, and mirror their behaviour.

'Burst-pulsed sounds are used in the life of bottlenose dolphins to socialise and maintain their position in the social hierarchy in order to prevent physical contact, and this also represents a significant energy saving.

'According to the experts, the tonal whistle sounds (the most melodious ones) allow dolphins to stay in contact with each other (above all mothers and offspring), and to coordinate hunting strategies. The burst-pulsed sounds (which are more complex and varied than the whistles) are used to avoid physical aggression in situations of high excitement, such as when they are competing for the same piece of food, for example.

'The dolphins emit these strident sounds when in the presence of other individuals moving toward the same

prey. The least dominant one soon moves away in order to avoid confrontation. The surprising thing about these sounds is that they have a high level of uni-directionality, unlike human sounds. One dolphin can send a sound to another that it sees as a competitor, and this one clearly knows it is being addressed.'

Now wait, I thought.

What these scientists were saying, if I was understanding it correctly, was that dolphins certainly could whistle – we've all heard them, right? – but that they can also use another type of sound that would be heard by only a single target dolphin.

Imagine humans who could speak to just one person in a crowded room – without shouting...

Just how much more advanced are these creatures?

I was puzzling over all that when the flight landed in Tampa. Dolphins drifted out of my mind temporarily, since the visit to Florida was supposed to be all about old gangsters and that sort of thing.

In truth, the 'boys' – as Sam referred to her father and uncle – hadn't seemed to me as if they'd ever been truly dangerous guys. In fact, they'd reminded me a lot of my own dad – a street fellow who had earned his way through school shooting billiards for tuition money. They brought back a lot of wonderful memories.

To be honest, I've screwed up a lot of things in my life – jobs, relationships, and so forth, and it was mostly because I hadn't grown up to be more like my dad. But I could never say things like that out loud. Nor would I mention anything about a plan to seek medical help from dolphins, either. Quite soon, however, I would find myself completely re-thinking that latter statement.

When it came time for bed that first night at John's house, I threw my duffel bag on a bed in the guest room and considered something you might call serendipity. The dolphin thing on the plane… recollections of my father…

Samantha believes in things like that – the feeling that you meet certain people for a reason. She kept reminding me that on the flight to Houston, we each had upgraded to first class. But we did it separately, and through completely different methods. She knew somebody working at the gate, and I was trying to use up a few of the airline's extra dividend miles.

That's how we had ended up sitting together, although this didn't automatically mean that the planet was going to shift on its axis. Sam, however, swears that everything is part of a plan.

I'm now inclined to look at some things her way – especially since I never did make it to any of Florida's dolphin parks. Instead, I wound up looking for one of those very same creatures a few thousand miles away.

Serendipity?

Staring out of the bedroom window at the Florida sky and listening to the sounds of the ocean just a block away, I laughed at my own imagination.

Silly me.

Chapter 4

Florida

August

To keep the right kind of flow in this strange and amazing tale, we now have to step back a few days. You see, something very curious happened even before I reached that rendezvous on Marco Island.

This part of the story involves automobiles, and something that was unprecedented throughout my entire career as a reporter and author.

I have long lost count of the number of rental cars that I've picked up while bounding around the United States and various parts of the world on assorted journalistic assignments. When snagging a hire vehicle, I always keep to the same routine. First I search for the car – which is usually in the last row. Then I toss my luggage into the boot and unfold a map for one more look at the best route to my destination. Then I switch on the mobile phone – which, of course, you must turn off during flights. I set the phone nearby on the passenger seat, together with a Diet Coke.

After that little ritual, I finally hit the road, singing along with country music crooner Willie Nelson: 'On the road again…'

And yes, I'd gone through that same song and dance at Tampa airport when I flew in for the drive south to meet Samantha and the brothers Vascuso. Or, I assumed that's what I'd done.

Normally I would let the air conditioner blast away during mid-summer in Florida, but a thunderstorm had blown through the Tampa area a couple of hours earlier and the air was surprisingly fresh. All I had to do was to roll down the windows and let that big, comfy luxury car do its thing on highway I-75.

It's only a couple of hours or so south to Marco Island, because even though cities like Fort Myers and Naples have grown from villages into massive shopping centres and residential developments, tourists pretty much stay away in the summer.

Although everywhere in the state is within half a day's drive of Disney World, Florida's habitually choked roads aren't very busy during hurricane season – unless residents are fleeing for their lives. Fortunately, on this particular trip, the Gulf Coast was calm and quiet.

As a matter of fact, inside the car itself was quiet. Too quiet. I should have noticed the silence before I got all the way to the turnoff for the bridge over to Marco Island. My phone hadn't made a peep. Since I always send out bulk e-mails to let clients, sources, editors and various other folk know where I'm going to be, calls generally come in bunches, or at the very least, once in a while. Nobody leaves you alone for nearly a full day, not in my kind of business.

I was whistling along with some music on the radio just north of the bridge near Marco when I finally realised that something wasn't right. I snatched up the phone and…

Yikes!

I discovered that I'd never turned the thing back on

after getting off my flight. So *that* was why it hadn't rung. Could the story of the decade have been assigned to somebody else while I was daydreaming?

It's a little strange to think about that now. At the time, the silence had seemed like a blessing.

As things developed, however, it turned out that I was just a day or two away from falling head-first into the most stunning adventure of my life. Who knows, if my phone had been switched on, and somebody had rung or sent me a text, things might have worked out quite differently. I might have been halted half way down the coast, checked a new message, and wound up doing interviews for Bo Tremaine, at a pottery show in the Arizona desert.

Yet things worked out exactly right, though of course at that point I had no idea about what was coming.

At the time, I was furious with myself. I'd been on hundreds of flights, and I'd never forgotten to switch on my mobile phone once on the ground... never. I have no doubt that Samantha would have called it fate, or the big plan, or some such, and maybe she'd have been right.

As it was, I pulled off the road into a parking space outside a pizza place, and checked for missed calls. There were six, which was a fairly light list considering my type of work. Four of them were expected, and that meant I could return them whenever I felt like it.

There were also a couple of calls from a number in Great Britain, country code 44 – and the digits weren't the least bit familiar. I have quite a few contacts in the UK, but most of them are in London, and all those numbers have a 20 prefix. This number wasn't one I remembered at all. For all I knew, it could have been a castle on the Isle of Skye.

I thought about ringing back to this strange new number, and saying something like, 'Cheers!'

But, no, I was already due to meet Samantha and her family down at the beach, and I decided that whoever was trying to ring me surely would give it another try sooner or later. Funny, because that call could have changed my schedule entirely. I have a vivid recollection of the whole scene even now. I can still smell the sausage pizza from just across the car park.

If that particular call had rung through while I was half way down the spine of Florida, I may well have phoned Sam with apologies and ignored Marco Island completely – especially with thoughts of dolphins already swimming about somewhere in the back of my mind. But I'll never know.

Right, now we're back up to date.

On my fourth morning in Florida, I was scribbling notes at John's kitchen table when my mobile phone beeped. Not a call this time, but a text message. Naturally, I'd managed to bury the phone under some stacks of paper, but at least it wasn't turned off. I scrambled around to find the mobile, checked the text… and discovered the same number that had appeared so mysteriously three days earlier.

The message said:

Where are you? Drop what you're doing and get here now. Biggest story you'll ever write. Ring me. Jill xxx

Oh, my…

It was a text from that onetime TV glamour girl Jill Gabriel, and I couldn't help but go a little dizzy. When I finally caught my breath, I tried to think. What in the world could make her jump out of whatever obscure bump in the road she'd been calling home to send me such a dramatic text?

I need to explain about Jill.

She had been a world-famous reporter for the BBC. Jill was born in London, but her background is a crazy mix of French, Persian, English and maybe even a little Native American. She was raised in the Kent countryside somewhere, but was at university in the States when her parents were killed in a hot air balloon accident. It turned out that their pilot had been high on opium, of all things, and the police took ages to clear the entire Gabriel family of suspected drug ties.

Jill had been furious. No, actually she was beyond furious. She went a bit crazy over the accusations, dropped out of school and dived into journalism, with a specific passion for crucifying every crooked cop, detective, inspector or other law enforcement officer in the known world. She found a tape of a chief superintendent doing 'naughty things' in a men's room, nailed an Irish customs official for taking bribes on deliveries of peat moss, and so on.

It had taken quite a few years for Jill to mellow out and turn into a respectable journalist. The funny thing was that after she'd wearied of the vendetta on behalf of her parents, she seemed startled to discover that she was just a really, really good reporter. And no one could miss that she was also a natural for television.

Jill is simply stunning, with long dark hair that almost ripples in different kinds of light, and deep, deep brown eyes that sometimes look like bottomless pools. She has a quizzical expression most of the time, and smiles only on special occasions – which is just as well, because it's the kind of look that makes drivers and pedestrians stop to gawp. Jill is a show-stopper. She was an automatic candidate for on-air talent from the day she first walked into a studio.

And here I must also confess that, yes, there was a romantic involvement in my case.

We'd met under circumstances that could only be called bizarre. Jill was a globe-trotting superstar who dated international kings of finance, and I was a scuffling journalist looking for a story, when we ran into each other in the ruins of Sarajevo. That was in 2001. I'd been fascinated by how the Serbs, Croats and Muslims had gone for each others' throats during the wholesale slaughter that lasted from 1992 to the beginning of '96.

I found the entire episode almost implausible, because I'd covered the Winter Olympics there in 1984 and thought that Sarajevo was just about the friendliest, most hospitable city in the world. Jill had come at it differently, of course, having become the *femme fatale* of war correspondents in Kashmir, Panama, Sri Lanka and anywhere else where gunfire was fashionable – until some barefoot Serb nearly shot her to pieces.

Anyway, I was back in Bosnia to write about rekindling hopes. She'd returned for a sobering little television piece on how, long after the war had ended, various factions were kept from killing each other only by the presence of UN troops. Oh, and she also hunted down the guy who had hollered 'Nice ass!' and saved her life a few years earlier. In fact, she'd bet him her car against his rifle that she could beat him in darts – and consequently was lugging around a loaded AK-47 when I met her in a little café where I had stopped to ask directions. I found out later that Jill had become disgusted by wars, and conflict in general, and that she'd made the wager only to take a weapon out of the kid's hands.

'You're the American writer,' Jill had said without any other introduction. 'Good piece you did on the romance of riverboats. I'd love to take a trip like that someday. Hey, can you field-strip an AK-47? I don't want to go round with this damn thing loaded.'

And so a friendship began – which later became a little more. In truth, it became *considerably* more.

I had no particular place to go once the Sarajevo story was finished, and Jill – here was a shock – had decided that she was just plain tired of the whole news industry. 'Show biz with dead bodies,' she called it.

For no reason worth remembering, we eventually went together to Switzerland and leased a cottage on a lake near Geneva. We stayed there through an entire snowy winter, building fires and talking about how the world really ought to be a better place.

By spring, we had agreed that the world was a lost cause, and our relationship, while not quite suffering from depletion of its ozone layer, perhaps needed a bit of air. We agreed to take a break and see how we felt about each other without war hangovers and Swiss fireplaces. Somehow we knew we'd meet again, but we were careful not to set a timetable.

I came back to the States. Jill disappeared to parts unknown, and had eventually landed in some way-out Scottish village, if I was reading the scrawl on her last postcard correctly. As far as I knew, she hadn't worked – or maybe even poked her head out in public – for several years. The BBC couldn't find her, and neither could anyone else.

If I'm honest, I'd missed her. A lot. But Jill isn't the type of person who can be pushed or hurried. When it was time, well, it would be time. She had sent me one other phone text, maybe a year earlier. All it had said was: *'Wind clears the soul. Threw the rifle into the sea. You'd look good in a kilt.'*

I had tried the phone number on that text, but it was a rental unit. So as far as I was concerned, she was lost without a trace.

And now, here I was loafing around Florida when, out of nowhere, Jill was back in my life – and delivering a summons. But it was not only that. Because I knew Jill so well, I could read between the beeps, so to speak. Whatever she'd found, it was pretty exciting.

So, with a major attack of nerves, I sat out by John Vascuso's pool in the broiling Florida sun and dialled the number in Britain. I expected a voicemail or something like that, because Jill never, ever answered her phone. But here came another shocker…

She picked it up straight away and got right to the point. 'Hello, there. Listen, forget the sunshine. There's a hug in this for you – but only if you can be in Glasgow tomorrow.'

I was too shocked to do anything but laugh.

At last I replied. 'Oh, sure. Are you watching from a satellite or something? How did you know I was someplace sunny? I'm actually not too far from Miami. But you didn't really know that… right?'

'Never mind all the geography,' she answered in a rush. 'This is better than anything you would ever guess. If you'll be sweet, and tell me you haven't slept a wink one single night without me, I might hand you the greatest story you're ever going to write.'

'You're serious.'

'Yep,' she replied. 'And I want you to meet someone.'

'Aw…you're not even alone.'

'I didn't say I'd be hugging anyone else,' she said.

'You sure?'

'My friend is eleven years old.'

Nearly half a minute went by in silence.

'Jilly, what's going on?' I asked. 'Be honest with me.'

'Please… just get a flight tonight. You'll understand

soon enough. Come to Glasgow and your world will never be the same. Have you ever known me to break a promise?'

'Only when you swore you'd leave the rifle in Bosnia.'

'Look, text me your flight information. I'll meet you. And as soon as I can arrange it, you need to see my friend Daisy. Oh, and before you leave, go online and look up a town in Scotland. Along with that hug, you even get to know where I live. I'll spell it for you: A-V-O-C-H.'

'A-vock?' I said, doing my best to try out the name phonetically.

'No, it's more like Och,' she corrected, stifling that tiny giggle that always made my heart do a funny little hop I remembered all too well. 'I've gotta run now. My battery's almost dead. I'll charge the phone. Text me. See you in Glasgow.'

Suddenly I felt frantic.

'Wait, Jill! I'm supposed to be going down to the Keys to see some dolphins and do a few other things. I...'

'Dolphins?' she repeated, with a little-girl gasp. 'You're kidding. Oh, Stephen, you're going to be *very* surprised.'

'Really?'

'We do have dolphins in Scotland, you know. Be a good boy, and Daisy will let you meet one.'

'Jilly, what are you talking about?'

'My battery's shot. Here's a kiss. See you at customs.'

Glasgow. Daisy. Dolphins. Now how would I explain this call to the Vascuso clan, without having them put me on medication? And how fast could I get to Miami?

I tried phoning Samantha's mobile to tell her what was going on, but reached her voicemail. I supposed she'd be at the gym.

'Hi, it's your hotshot journalist,' I said after the beep. 'I'll try you again, but I've got to take off this afternoon to catch a flight. John and Tommy have been great. I'll fill you in from the airport. Say hi to Jim... and the kids... and the mice. Bye.'

Trying to take stock of a very strange situation, I strolled slowly back into the house.

'Fellas,' I said, 'something crazy has come up. And I can't really explain it because I don't really know what's going on. But I've got to be on the other side of the world. Like, now...'

Instantly, they jumped into action. This was exactly their kind of situation. Leap on planes, search for strangers in odd places...

'I want your job,' Tommy announced.

I addressed them both. 'Believe me, guys. Honestly, I don't know what it's all about. But I do have to go to Scotland.'

John smirked. 'There's a woman in this. There's got to be.'

They both started laughing.

'Yeah,' Tommy agreed. 'Who'd run out on us if it didn't have something to do with a lady?'

Chapter 5

En route to Scotland

August

I don't remember too much of the drive to Miami.

Normally it's a trip I'd find amusing, if only to note how crazy some patches of America must seem to a first-time visitor. Highway 41 from Marco Island marches pretty much straight east through the Everglades – past a couple of Indian casinos, the Miccosukee Reservation, assorted alligator farms and various trinket shops selling genuine swampland artefacts, made in Taiwan. Just as you reach the outskirts of the Miami metro area, a quick jaunt south on Route 997 would put you in easy reach of the Metrozoo, Fruit and Spice Park, Monkey Jungle, Orchid Jungle, the Coral Castle and Homestead Miami Speedway.

After that, you run out of land and begin the long jaunt out along the Keys on A1A. Then it's about 180 miles to Key West – where Hemingway once housed hundreds of cats – and the next stop after that is Havana. That's the direction I'd originally been planning to go, most likely to one of the dolphin parks in Key Largo, or even an hour further on to the Dolphin Research Centre at Grassy Key.

This time, though, I gave a little salute, roared past the turnoff, and waded straight into the monstrous, multicultural mess that is greater Miami. Unless you're a South Beach cross-dresser, or part of the massive and politically aggressive Cuban population, there really isn't much charm left in Miami. Even the flamingos at old Hialeah race track have been sent scurrying off, with the place earmarked for some sort of new development.

The best drive in Miami is the one I was making that particular noontime – straight to the airport to dump a rental car and hop on a flight out. All of this is easier said than done, of course. Miami has more petty thieves – and dangerous ones, as a matter of fact – than anywhere in the free world. It's not unusual to be relieved of your wallet at knifepoint, within yards of the rental car check-in counter.

A friend of mine spent five years working for a Miami newspaper, and was robbed seven times, always with a weapon involved. By pure chance he never was shot, stabbed, clubbed or garrotted while handing over his $10 or whatever loose change came to hand. But eventually he decided that the odds were getting a little short, and took off for a quiet desk job in Omaha.

The sweetest sound in Miami is that roar of the jet engines as you hurtle down the runway en route to somewhere else. Even the back alleys of Calcutta seem like sleepy suburban neighbourhoods by comparison. Assuming that you still have your wallet, keys, money, passport, watch, and anything else that could have been lifted in the previous hour or so, it's always a treat to lean back and watch the skyline of Miami disappear in favour of the endless blue Atlantic.

Now, safely installed on my flight, I let my mind drift off wherever it cared to go. And that, naturally, took me to Jill and Switzerland. No matter what craziness she was talking about so excitedly on the phone, I would be seeing her again.

So I smiled, and felt a warm glow of expectation. No use denying that.

I had to deal with a change of planes in New York, because I couldn't get a direct flight to Glasgow – despite non-stop pleading with a vicious woman clerk who was hoarding seats for passengers far, far beyond their assigned check-in time. Typical Miami hospitality. Why on earth do Europeans continue to visit this place? Ah, well, after the enforced hour layover in New York, the rest of my time would be free for letting my active imagination run wild.

When I'd phoned Samantha from the airport in Miami – while simultaneously strong-arming a bum who was begging for spare change in three languages – she had sounded wildly enthusiastic about the shocking call from Jill, the mystery of little Daisy and the cryptic references to dolphins.

'What an adventure!' she had shouted. 'Ooh, I wish I were going along. Don't worry. We'll sort out the boys' show when you get back. Bring me home some Chivas Regal, okay?'

I still felt a little guilty, and pressed her on the issue of my having just left Marco Island and her family so abruptly.

'They were great to me,' I told her. 'I wish I could get half their stories printed without needing an army of libel lawyers. You sure you feel okay with this dash to Scotland? Jill wouldn't make a call like this if it weren't something special. It's just not her style. With Jill, it's got to be huge or she doesn't bother. She'd rather sit on the beach.'

Samantha was resolute. 'Don't explain another thing. You might be heading off to write the book of your life.

But you're also going to see a pretty special woman again, right?'

'True,' I admitted.

'Then it's settled,' Sam concluded. 'A good woman should always come first. Take it from another good woman.'

Why hadn't my ex-wife been so reasonable about the here-today, gone-tomorrow demands of journalism? Perhaps I should have brought up the subject *before* we mumbled our vows, instead of breaking the news after a 3 a.m. phone call from Hong Kong that arrived two weeks into married life. Shame about that...

I would have plenty of time to wonder about Jill, the dolphins and Daisy before I landed in Glasgow at 8.30 the next morning. The child certainly was a wild card, because I couldn't recall Jill ever talking much about kids. Oh, and Avoch – pronounced 'Och'.

I found a pay-as-you-go internet station in the airport, and located Avoch. It certainly was a long way up in the north of Scotland – nowhere near Glasgow – and it was sitting on a body of water that was either the Beauly Firth or the Moray Firth, depending on how you interpreted the map. In either case, both emptied into the North Sea. I had a few minutes to fiddle around with two or three websites before giving up, but couldn't find much more information on Avoch – except that it obviously wasn't very big, and there was a mention of dolphin-spotting boats departing from the tiny harbour nearby.

It seemed that now, every time I turned round, I found another pod of dolphins. That notion made me smile – as dolphins always do – and I dozed off in a mood of light-heartedness, my thoughts wandering freely, on the flight up to New York.

On the Glasgow leg of the journey, though, reality began to set in, and I gave myself a headache while trying to sort out what puzzle Jill Gabriel possibly might be trying to solve, and how it involved me. It would be lovely to believe that she just missed my winning charm, but...

Thinking of Jill is normally quite a pleasant experience. Amazingly, we had almost no disagreements, snits, arguments or anything of the sort during our time together. We went in different directions comfortably, friends forever, probably both guessing that there was another warm and fuzzy chapter to come.

The hardest thing to explain, when friends cared to ask, was why we split in the first place. I'd never really spent much time revisiting the heart of it – which was that we both had unfinished business elsewhere, though neither of us knew what that might be. I certainly didn't have any idea what I intended to do, professionally or otherwise. And that's been the story of my life, more or less. I suspect that Jill was just as clueless about the where, what, why and all the rest of it for herself.

I felt I could assume that she'd finished with the job of documenting human conflict and misery, because she'd seen so much of it – not to mention getting shot. I'd be shocked if someone had lured her back into that game. As for stepping back into the public eye, well, I had no idea. My best guess would be that she had been looking to do something 'important', but wouldn't have been able to name what it was until she found it.

The day we said good-bye at the Geneva train station, we each tried to guess what we'd do next, and how we'd hear of each other again. It was mostly for laughs because, deep down, we understood we were parting, and each of us knew that we would be lonely for a while – perhaps a longer time than we wished.

Finally we had decided that we'd each scribble down one prediction concerning the other's future, and agreed that we wouldn't read them until we were apart.

I had written: 'You'll run for the British House of Commons and win. Women will take you seriously, and men will vote for your legs.'

It had been more than a day into my post-Geneva journey – first to Paris, then a flight home to the States – before I unfolded the little piece of café napkin on which Jill had written her guess about me. I remember feeling a little nervous, waiting to read what she'd seen in her crystal ball. I was sure that it would be something light and breezy, but I was wrong.

Her note said: 'You'll write lots of silly things that make millions of people happy, and then one big thing that changes their lives.'

I had stashed the frayed slice of napkin in a plastic sheath that same day, tucked it into my passport folder, and I'd carried it with me every minute of the years that had trickled away since we'd said good-bye.

When the flight attendant brought tea about an hour into the flight to Glasgow, I fished out Jill's note and read it again. I shivered – couldn't help it. I had absolutely no idea what the lady was doing, but I was sure as the Scots make scones that she thought the time had come for her prediction to be fulfilled.

Jilly, where are you taking us? All I knew was that we'd be starting in Scotland, so on a dash through the gift shop just before flight time in New York, I went looking for reading material. The best I could do was a book about William Wallace, the Scottish martyr made famous by actor Mel Gibson in the film 'Braveheart'.

Wallace was a nationalist who galvanized what had been a rag-tag gang of Scots into a serious fighting force. His army won some heroic battles against the overwhelming might of England. In the end, Wallace was captured, and not only executed, but also parts of his body were put on display all over the country. There's nothing like a subtle reminder to the populace about the penalty for disagreement with the monarchy.

I already knew Wallace's story, of course, but I nearly dumped tea all over my lap when I read about a man called Andrew Murray – 'the other Braveheart' – who had fought a fierce war of resistance against the English in Scotland's Gaelic north. Murray's Highlanders drew serious blood in the 1290s, and later he joined forces with the lowland leader Wallace.

Together they overran the English at the Battle of Stirling Bridge in September of 1297, though apparently Murray was mortally wounded. Reports are sketchy, but clearly he died within weeks of the victory. Timing is everything, even when creating movie heroes.

Wallace fought on until captured, and he remains one of Scotland's most famous sons. In August of 2005, a few thousand Scots staged an honorary funeral procession for Wallace on the streets of London – marking the 700th anniversary of his death and his final cry of 'Freedom!'

Pausing for a minute, I recalled that the Scotlandish Parliament now was controlled by the SNP – Scottish National Party – and that there would be a vote on independence from the United Kingdom coming in 2014. Current polls suggested that Scots would vote to remain loyal to Westminster, but my mother was raised in Scotland, and I know first-hand that my ancestors can be an unpredictable lot.

I went back to my studying. Murray seemed to have been every bit as much a hero as the now-famous Wallace, and once escaped an English prison. After he slipped out of the dungeon at Chester Castle, Murray launched a guerrilla campaign, rallying Highlanders in the north to his cause and terrorising the English occupation forces for years. Murray's crusade, which was one of the proudest and bloodiest in Scottish history, began in the town of…

Avoch.

Suddenly I felt too warm in the plane seat, and felt a sudden need to walk up and down the aisle for a few minutes. I tried to make sense of this new information as I strolled through the darkened cabin.

Now why had I grabbed *that* book off the shelf? Jill, please tell me the name of the town is just an odd little coincidence. Really. This isn't Northern Ireland. The SNP has tea in London. This can't be about an angry splinter group or any of that nonsense. No way. And whatever you're up to, how in heaven's name could an eleven-year-old girl be in the middle of it?

'Och,' she had said.

I barely slept a wink all the way to Glasgow. Jill had kept me awake until dawn before, but never like this. The only thing that made me laugh, just as we were descending into what looked like a typical grey and misty Scottish morning, was remembering the prediction that I'd written on her little slip of paper nearly ten years ago in Geneva. Jill in the House of Commons? I must have suffered a sugar rush from too much Swiss chocolate before I wrote that note.

That's what was wandering through my mind as the wheels touched down. What on Earth might be going on with Jill, and with the little girl whom she seemed to believe might change our lives?

I'd made the leap, so there was nothing to do but face the chilly morning and find some answers. Knowing Jill Gabriel, though, I was absolutely positive that there was an adventure in front of us. But of what sort, I had no idea.

Chapter 6

International Arrivals Terminal
Glasgow

Late August

When we'd touched down in Scotland, I felt groggy from the all-night trek across the Atlantic, a five-hour change on my watch, and barely a wink of sleep. There was a delay of some sort once we were on the ground – and of course there's always plenty of time standing around in the usual mob scene at immigration and customs.

Naturally I was wondering about Jill. I was trying hard not to shiver at the notion that I'd shortly be seeing her for the first time in years. And her exclamation about dolphins when I'd mentioned the subject during our hurry-up phone call...

Why all this fuss?

Now that I'd put aside my plan to see if those amazing mammals in Florida might do something about the pain in my shoulders, I tried to piece together what I knew and remembered of dolphins in general. One specific memory came rushing back from maybe twenty years earlier, when I'd been living in California.

My mom had died of a heart seizure. It had been a horrible time. Not only had she collapsed suddenly just a

44

few days before Christmas, but also I had found her myself on the floor of her bedroom. My dad had been a victim of colon cancer twelve years before that. My sister was married and living more than an hour away, so as the only remaining family member, I had no choice but to put my career on hold, move into Mom's house and make it presentable for sale. It was a grim and depressing stretch of months.

The entire process of unloading the house stretched out over more than six months. I tried to do some magazine writing during the wait, but my head wasn't really into it, and I recall wasting a lot of days just lying outside, soaking up sun on the back deck, and wondering what the hell I was going to do once the house was sold.

Coincidentally, there was a young woman living next door who'd gone through a tough time of her own. Cathy had been pushed into a divorce – abandoned would be a better description – and in addition to working full-time, she spent the rest of her hours taking care of two kids and her mother. She didn't really have a chance to get out much – a shame, because she was fun, charming and full of life. She always seemed to be scrambling for chances to do things with her son and daughter – a cheerful pair who were happy for company just about any time.

I didn't really have any kind of schedule to keep, unless there were prospective buyers coming to see the house, so I made Cathy a standing offer to take her and the kids off for a picnic or some other outing – whenever she could find a little time. We managed to squeeze in a few enjoyable days, taking sandwiches to some pretty spot in the hills and visiting the zoo in San Francisco.

Once, Cathy and I spent a full afternoon at a unique theme park in a suburb called Redwood City. I remember thinking it was a shame that her kids weren't with us, but they were away with a friend's family that day. The complex was actually two parks in one. There was a section called Africa USA and also an aquatic centre that drew crowds to shows with leaping dolphins, a famous whale and performing seals. But the most intriguing attraction of the aquatic centre was a dolphin petting pool.

I'd already visited 'routine' dolphin shows, of course, and was amazed yet again at the grace and timing of creatures that seemed able to fling themselves fifteen to twenty feet into the air with perfect precision. Standing at the petting pool, however, was the first time I'd ever seen a dolphin up close. In fact, the three or four animals swimming around in the shallow water came right up to the low concrete wall of their enclosure. They seemed to enjoy being stroked, and sometimes would roll over for a bit of a tummy rub. The experience was enchanting. I can't think of any other word to describe it.

We spent at least an hour at the dolphin pool, and there I witnessed something stunning that has stayed in my mind ever since.

The chain of events started when a girl of about twelve years old began playing with one particular dolphin. Clearly both of them were enjoying it a lot, and the dolphin kept popping up out of the water to squeak and whistle with obvious approval as the girl clapped and patted him.

Kids being kids, two boys around fifteen or sixteen wandered on to the scene, and after watching this little girl and the dolphin for a bit, they started making some rude remarks. They teased the girl, and then laughed at her, suggesting that the dolphin couldn't tell one person from another – and that she'd only found her new 'friend' because she'd fed the dolphin from a little carton of fish she'd bought near the pool.

At first the girl ignored these two clowns, but they kept at it, and finally one of them tugged at her hair. The other one made some silly remark that was vaguely directed at the dolphin. I recall that the girl was trying very hard not to cry, but there was no one around to help her, and the boys were becoming more and more obnoxious.

One of the guys said, 'That fish doesn't know you. He just wanted the food and now he doesn't have anyplace else to go. He's just a dumb fish staring at a dumb girl!'

At that point, I decided get involved and have a word with these two characters. But before I'd taken three or four steps towards them, the dolphin suddenly ducked his head and disappeared under the water.

'Look, he's gone and left you,' one of the boys said, letting out an unpleasant hoot.

A moment later, though, we all stood and stared, because the dolphin had reappeared, emerging from the water upside down. All we could see was this huge tail – which for a second or two, seemed to fill the entire sky.

There was a heartbeat of silence, and then suddenly the dolphin lashed that mighty tail downward with thunderous force – whomp! A mountain of water buried the two boys, who were drenched from head to foot before they could even take a step.

The girl, who remained perfectly dry, even though she was just a few feet away from the watery explosion, simply stood with her mouth open. Then she began to giggle. And a few seconds later, the dolphin emerged once more – upright this time – and began cackling so loudly that you could hear it all the way across the park.

There was no denying what we'd seen. This dolphin, having a good old time with a new pal, clearly had reacted to the interruption. Deciding that the boys were acting like bullies, he had turned his body 180 degrees under the water, and covered them with gallons of water. And then he had returned to laugh about it with the girl.

The dolphin's decision to defend his new friend with a little prank seemed terrific enough, but it was almost eerie how he'd managed to direct that huge splash of water so accurately while turned completely upside down. No one around the pool except the two boys was hit by a single drop.

I wondered then, and for quite a while afterwards, just how the dolphin had been able to pull off such a feat. I knew that it was just a bit of fun and all that. But how much of what had been said at the edge of the pool had the dolphin actually understood? How had he chosen that particular act of retribution? And how in the world could he direct a fifteen-foot cascade of water with such accuracy, when his head was almost touching the bottom of the pool?

'I wonder how the dolphin knew that nobody up above him had moved?' my friend said. 'If they'd each just taken a few steps, it could have been the girl who got soaked.'

Although we couldn't be absolutely sure, Cathy and I both thought that we had seen the dolphin hesitate – almost as though he were aiming his tail – before banging it down on to the surface. I'd never seen anything quite like it.

I was mulling over that memory, still shuffling through the immigration lines at Glasgow airport, when it dawned on me that I'd never worked out a proper explanation of that incident so long ago.

What exactly *are* dolphins capable of doing?

By now I had just about reached the smiling lady official who would welcome me back to the United Kingdom, ask nonchalantly if I might be a member of any known terrorist organisation and then, satisfied that I posed no serious security risk to Queen or country, would bang a new stamp into my passport book.

48

Barely conscious of all the formalities, I was staring at nothing in particular, and wondering if Jill actually might have information that would fill in some blanks about dolphins and their capabilities.

Oh, how that thought turned out to be a massive underestimate.

Chapter 7

Glasgow to Auchterarder

Late August, morning

I nearly missed Jill at the Glasgow arrivals hall. I was a little bleary from flying all night, but the possibility that I wouldn't spot Jill Gabriel almost instantly had never crossed my mind.

So I wandered through the usual crowd of families, exhausted travellers and the mass of staff, looking all over the place for that familiar face somewhere in the mob. Then it dawned on me, just for a second, that perhaps somehow I'd misunderstood the plan. After all, Jill's message had been brief and hurried. Maybe she'd been delayed, or had changed her mind and wasn't going to turn up at all.

My stomach was beginning to hop around in a very uncomfortable way, when I heard a voice almost directly behind me.

'Hey, there. Looking for someone?'

Oh, my... no wonder I'd walked right past her. Jill was decked out in a tartan skirt, with a matching little cap and snow-white sweater. She looked like a model in a merchandise catalogue. And she was wearing make-up, which she never did – except on TV. Jill's everyday outfits had consisted of army fatigue jackets, jeans and boots. In summer, or in Africa, she replaced the jacket with a wrinkled T-shirt.

My jaw must have dropped, because Jill started giggling and said, 'Wanted something a little rougher, did you?'

I had to laugh.

'All you need is some knee-high socks and you'd be ready to break out in a Highland fling,' I told her. 'What's with the fashion show?'

Jill actually blushed. And that startled me, as well, because I'm sure I'd never once seen her blush for any reason at all.

'Um, I didn't want you to think I'd gone to seed, or been living with goats in the Himalayas,' she replied, still smiling. 'And... well, I thought maybe I should try to look... nice. You know?'

For the record, yes, she looked nice. *Very* nice.

After what seemed like an eternity, Jill finally took a couple of steps forward and wrapped me in a hug that was followed by a kiss. Not a movie-scene kiss exactly, but I still felt a tingle all the way up my spine.

'Miss me?' she asked.

'Guess.'

'Thank goodness,' she replied. 'I can quit worrying and dump this little "lassie" outfit as soon as we get home. You know, it's been a while, Stephen. I really did wonder if you truly wanted to see me again, or whether you would just come running because of a great story.'

I'd thought about that myself, and I knew darn well how much I wanted to see her – probably more than it was wise to admit. But I was also certainly hooked by the mystery of whatever was going on. Even the seriously lovesick don't simply ring up and demand that their sweeties fly halfway round the world in less than 24 hours.

It was time to find out what was happening with Miss Jill.

So I asked, 'What's the story? You hauled me off Marco Island, where I was getting a very nice tan and talking to a couple of great guys about a magazine story I think maybe I could sell. You sounded like you've fallen over some news, or information, or whatever, that might make the world stop spinning...'

'Maybe I have.'

'Seriously?'

'Yes, and please note I didn't ring anybody else. I do know a few dozen good reporters and writers, remember?'

'I'm flattered. And yes, I'm really, um... thrilled to see you. Thrilled, and then some, okay?'

'We sound like a couple of teenagers talking about going steady. Shall we agree it'll be nice to hang around together again, and just go from there?'

'I'd like that.'

'Good boy. We can talk about everything in the car, but I really and truly meant it when I said this might be the biggest story of your life – of both our lives, in fact.'

'Whoa!'

'I've never been more serious about news, or whatever we decide to call this. Stephen, this is really, really something special.'

'So tell me,' I said with a sigh that might have come out with a tiny hint of frustration. 'I've been awake all night, listening to a baby cry in the row beside me, and worrying that maybe you've found some way back into the violence business. I even read a book about an old Scottish revolutionary from...'

'Avoch.'

She pronounced it 'Och', as she had on the phone.

'Well, lady, you got famous telling millions of people about bombs and massacres and rocket-propelled grenades

– not to mention terrorists. It's pretty natural that something like that might cross my mind, don't you think?'

'Och, aye,' she answered, using a Scottish idiom for the first time. 'But I'm out of the shooting business – past and present. I'm as far out of it as you can get. What I want to show you is light-years from that, believe me. If there's something that's the complete opposite of violence, this might be it.'

'Well, you didn't exactly come dressed like a war correspondent, I'll concede that. I never thought I'd imagine the words "Jill" and "cute" in the same sentence, but…'

She burst into laughter and said, 'C'mon, we've got to find some people in a town up the road. One of them is a little girl I met on the beach. I want you to hear what she has to say. Then you can decide if leaving your cushy Florida assignment was worth the effort.'

I was thinking that this vision of Jill – brilliant, gorgeous Jill – was worth the effort already. But I kept silent on that one.

'Nae worries,' I told her. 'I just wish I had a camera. Your old pals at the BBC would pay plenty for a shot of you dressed up to dance with some fiddlers.'

Still holding on to her stop-traffic smile, Jilly just shook her head and grabbed my hand. 'Have you any luggage besides that one case?'

'Nope.'

'Well, this isn't Florida, my boy. Good thing I'm always prepared. I bought you a leather jacket – very posh, I might add – and a couple of sweaters. Some Brits call them jumpers, by the way. That'll keep you from freezing for now, and we can go shopping when we get up north.'

So we made our way through the airport, and out into

the cold and misty Glasgow morning. We wandered around for a bit as Jill tried to remember where she'd parked.

'I don't drive much,' she admitted as we marched up one row of cars and back down the next. 'I can walk anywhere I need to go in Avoch, or up to the village of Fortrose. You'll get to know that road. And there's always a bus to Inverness for real shopping. The last time I had to drive anywhere was when I was catching a flight to London, and then on to Brazil. It's funny, you can just about see the Inverness airport from my cottage, but it's way over on the other side of the firth and it's really a long way round to it. You'll understand the geography when you see the area.'

Jill's car was a little purple thing, which she told me was a Corsa – a make you'd never see in America, where everyone is still buying giant SUVs and running pedestrians off the roads.

Having bundled us into the vehicle, Jill found her way to the exit after a couple of near misses. I suddenly recalled why I did all the necessary driving during our time in Switzerland. But Jill seemed to relax once on the open road, and finally, she let out a deep breath.

'I'm so glad you're here,' she said.

'Mmmm...'

'It isn't just... you know... us? I really, really wanted to see you, Stephen. I waited too long. I missed you. I did. But I wasn't kidding about the story, either. You're the only person I'd ever call about this.'

'So you did think of me once in a while, maybe?'

I was fishing for a compliment, of course, and the Jill Gabriel I'd known normally would have returned something snappy, putting me straight in my place – but instead she responded... girlishly.

'I'll tell you something kind of embarrassing, and then

let's drop the stupid stuff and just be us,' she replied.

'Right.'

'Okay, I actually checked to see if you were married or had a serious woman in your life.'

'You're kidding.'

Jill blushed again. That was the second time in just a few minutes. Amazing.

'I paid an agency to find you and e-mail me a report,' she admitted. 'Oh... I can't believe I'm telling you this.'

I felt just wonderful. Wisely, however, I kept my mouth shut.

Jill continued briskly. 'Anyway, now you know, and I'm finished feeding your ego and playing the Bogart-Hepburn routine. If you want to talk more about us – as in *us* – we'll have plenty of time up in Avoch. But first we're going to a town called Auchterarder, to a fantastic little tea shop that has the best apple pie in the world.'

I grinned, and she whipped her head toward me.

'Don't smirk like that!' she hissed, in a voice that I knew so very well. 'It's great pie, and it's an easy place to meet them.'

'Them?'

Jill ignored me, took a breath and continued as though she'd been practising this speech, maybe working on it for hours. Our little romantic teasing was over.

'I want you to meet my friend Daisy and her mother,' she explained. 'I saw Daisy at a place called Chanonry Point, up by Fortrose. She's eleven years old, although sometimes I think she seems wise enough to be a hundred.'

'Daisy.'

'Daisy Paisley. And don't you dare laugh. Her mother's name is Maisie, believe it or not, but everyone calls her Edy.'

'But what are they doing in Auchterarder? That can't

be next door to Avoch and the Black Isle.'

'Edy's sister lives in Auchterarder, and they're visiting her,' Jill explained patiently.

'Ah, so that explains the choice of pie shop.'

Jill smiled.

'Daisy Paisley…' I repeated, almost to myself.

'Yes,' said Jill, 'and why Edy gave her kid a name like that, I've no idea. But Daisy gets enough stick about the name from kids at school, so just be nice.'

'Stick?'

'Oh, Stephen. You Yanks don't get out much. In Britain, giving someone "stick" is like giving them grief, or kidding them.'

'Stick.' I savoured the word and then said, 'Right, so I'm going to meet a girl named Daisy and her mother. I'll just leave Daisy's last name out and forget I ever heard it. Now why would I want to talk to this particular eleven-year-old?'

Jill fell silent. I'd been around her enough to remember this special sort of pause. She was searching for the precise way to explain whatever was coming next, so I waited.

Then I saw a sign for a layby up ahead, and to my surprise, she slowed the car and drew into it.

She turned and looked at me straight in the face. 'Just listen for now,' she said, sounding a bit like a school teacher.

'Right.'

'Okay, you're in Scotland this morning because Daisy has been talking to a dolphin.'

There was stone-dead silence in the car. I had no response to give. I tried to process where she was going, realised I couldn't, and simply waited for her to continue the story.

'Really and truly, she's been talking to a dolphin," Jill

said quietly, realising the implication of her statement. 'She trusts me, and she's told me quite a lot about it. And... and I believe her.'

What could I say to that? At last I settled on a question. 'How does Daisy, uh, talk to this dolphin? Do they have a sign language or something?'

'No,' said Jill, her voice dropping almost to a whisper. 'They talk kind of like we talk. "How are you? I'm fine." That kind of talk.'

'You're saying that the dolphin actually speaks to her? In plain English?'

'Oh, wait, no,' Jill replied. 'It's not that simple. Daisy told me the dolphin can say some words out loud, and that she can understand him – but with some difficulty, I gather. When he speaks that way, it's difficult and squeaky, so...'

'So?'

'He speaks directly into her mind.'

I opened my mouth to comment, but Jill cut me off and continued. 'Now before you say anything or make a face, let me finish. I know you've always loved dolphins and have an interest in them, so you've seen and read enough to understand that they have these amazing abilities with echolocation. It's been proven that they can "scan" us and know our moods – how we feel, things like that. And lots of people go to swim with dolphins because they can sort of buzz you. It's a much more refined version of our medical ultrasound treatments – healing aches, curing joint pains and so forth.'

I decided not to mention, at least right then, that I had been planning to try exactly that same sort of procedure with some dolphins in Florida to get help with my shoulders. Jill was rolling along with her story, and I didn't want to interrupt her.

'Well, apparently their abilities are way, way more

complex and sophisticated than that,' she said. 'Daisy told me that dolphins actually can read our minds, and if we want to communicate something specifically, they can answer. I've been checking on this and reading material from various researchers, and they all seem to agree that the idea of a dolphin picking up on what you're thinking or saying isn't far-fetched at all. But so far, nobody has suggested that they can respond directly in language that a human can understand. I suppose they do it by using some form of their echolocation, which creates the sentence or thought, and they send it clearly to a person who is listening for it.

'Daisy talks to the dolphin that way, and she's been doing it for a few months. She speaks out loud, asking a question or something, and she hears a clear, comprehensible answer – except that there's no audible sound. Not audible to her, or anyone else. The closest thing I can imagine to it would be something like ESP. But these aren't just general thoughts or feelings. They're fully formed sentences, and Daisy says she has no trouble understanding this dolphin at all. Isn't that wild?'

'Well, that's one word that comes to mind.'

'You don't believe it.'

'I didn't say that. I'm reserving judgment for the moment. But I'd *love* to believe it.'

Jill started the car, and once back on the road she continued the story as she steered the little Corsa north past Stirling on the A9.

'I wouldn't have phoned you way over in America, and begged you to get here in a few hours just because of a little girl's story,' she assured me. 'Oh, damn, maybe I would, because I was wondering how I was going to find a way to see you again. But I didn't in this case. I did not.'

'So there's more…'

'Yes, one thing. Last week, Daisy told the dolphin

that I was her friend and that she thought I believed her about their conversations, and she asked if he would let me come with her to see him.'

'And...?'

'I guess the dolphin said he didn't mind. So on Friday evening I went with her to this place called Chanonry Point that I mentioned earlier. Actually, it's well known for dolphin-watching, because lots of them swim right past it. It has to do with tides or something, but the dolphins like the water there, and they hang around the Point, sometimes for hours. Anyway, I went along and we saw several dolphins, and it wasn't even two minutes before one of them swam right up near us and stopped with his head out of the water.

'Right away, Daisy said, "Hi, this is Jill, my friend. She used to be a famous television person." The dolphin made a funny squeaking noise, and Daisy laughed. Then she turned to me and said: "He asked me if they decided you were too old to be on television any more."

'I felt like I was in a dream. I asked Daisy if the dolphin really had spoken those exact words to her and she said, "Of course. That's how we talk. But I know he was just joking about your age."

'I was speechless, Stephen. For a moment I wondered if the girl was making up the whole thing, that she'd been imagining conversations all along, and that I'd somehow got hooked into a kind of prank. But before I could do anything else, Daisy spoke out loud to the dolphin again, and she was very clear. She asked if he would speak to me so I'd know she wasn't just fooling around.'

Here Jill paused, and suddenly I realised a couple of things. The first was that I'd been holding my breath, like you do right before the big moment at a great movie or something. The second was that Jill had pulled the car off to the side of the road so that she could look straight at me.

'What happened?' I asked, thinking that maybe I already knew the answer.

'Stephen, you know me – maybe better than anyone does. No, definitely better than anyone. I'm the person who wouldn't report on battle casualties until I'd counted the bodies myself.

'I'm not a dreamer, and I'm not nuts.'

'And…'

'And the dolphin looked right at me and I think he said "Hello" – except I'm sure he didn't make any kind of sound. I just, like, heard him in my head. And all I could think of to say was, "Thank you." '

Jill looked at me for a long time, as though waiting to be interrogated, or have her sanity questioned.

Finally, I asked, 'Is there any more?'

'A little,' she replied. 'I spoke out loud directly to the dolphin and asked him if I could talk to him a bit more. And pretty clearly, inside my head I'm sure – well, pretty sure – I heard him answer: "Later."

'And that was it. What I remember was that it seemed very clear, as though he was speaking aloud, but there were other people around, and it was obvious that none of them heard or noticed anything. Daisy spoke to the dolphin again, just for a minute or two, and then she said that we should go, but that she absolutely had to meet me the next morning.

'That was last Saturday, and Daisy came to my cottage. She seemed a little different, almost like she was in a trance – still fine, but just different somehow. Usually when she visits we have tea, but she decided she'd rather not have anything. She told me that she had a message for me, and wanted to concentrate on getting it right.

'I can't remember her exact words, but the point was very clear. The dolphin wanted her to bring me back again. But the big thing was that she had a very exact request from him. He wanted me to contact a media person whom I trusted more than anyone in the world, someone from Britain or America only, and that I should introduce that person to Daisy.

'I asked Daisy then what it was all about, but she just said it would be better if I found the right person, and then she would talk to both of us at the same time. She said she hoped I could do it soon, because the dolphin told her it was very, very important.'

By this time we were coming up to the turn for Auchterarder. I'd looked up the place on her map and discovered it was right near the famous Gleneagles resort. Under normal circumstances, I'd have been wishing I had my golf clubs with me, but needless to say, golf didn't even cross my mind this time.

'We're supposed to meet Daisy and Edy in a few minutes,' Jill announced. 'You've been up flying all night, Stephen, and now I'm telling you a story that sounds like science fiction. Are you up to this?'

'I think so,' I replied, trying to sound calm and confident.

Jill was idling down the long main street that comprises most of Auchterarder, looking for a place to park, when a question came to me out of nowhere.

'Hey, this dolphin of Daisy's... does she call him anything special? I mean, does he have a name?'

'Oh, I guess I just went right by that,' she answered, with a laugh that came out a little nervously. 'His name is Spike.'

Okay, so I was going off to have tea with an eleven-year-old girl who spoke with a dolphin named Spike. There was nothing else to say. Not right then.

Chapter 8

Auchterarder

Late August, midday

First of all, just to break the suspense a little bit, I am very glad to be able to report that the apple pie was as good as advertised.

Our unusual little group of four sat at a corner table, away from whatever crowds of local gossip-mongers might hang around the place. After formal introductions, which seemed easy and comfortable under the circumstances, we came to some kind of unspoken agreement to order our tea and pastries, talk about the weather – always a good topic in Scotland – and sit around as though we'd known each other forever and had just happened to drop in for a regular midday chat.

Not a word was said about Daisy's dolphin experience while we ate, and much to Jill's delight I ordered a second go-round on the pie.

Meanwhile, I tried for a quick study of the Paisleys. Mum was clearly a proper Scottish countrywoman, full of good health and cheer. Whether or not she knew the actual purpose of our meeting, I couldn't tell.

Jill had mentioned that she knew Edy Paisley, but not well. They'd exchanged all the usual hellos along the road in Avoch, borrowed sugar and such from each other, and appeared pleased with each other's presence, but I'm sure that Jill was wondering – as I was – if Daisy had shared any of her dolphin revelations with her mother. And if so, how much?

Had the girl been telling her parents all along what was going on during her visits to Chanonry Point, and, more to the point, what did they believe? For all we knew, Daisy had been chattering away at home about how exciting she found her conversations with Spike and, if that were the case, maybe Mum and Dad thought that the girl needed counselling.

Yet somehow it didn't feel that way, either because Daisy had been keeping Spike as her private pal, or because the parents simply dismissed the tales as the harmless adventures of an eleven-year-old kid living in a Highlands coastal village without much else to do but spend time with an imaginary friend.

Actually, there was a third possibility. Perhaps she had told her parents chapter and verse about her visits to see Spike, and they were open-minded enough that they considered the stories, or some version of them, to carry a bit of truth.

Daisy's father, I learned, had run a fishing boat from the Black Isle harbour of Cromarty, until some nagging heart problems had forced him into less vigorous employment at a local bank. If William Paisley – finally, a normal name – had spent much of his life on the sea, in an area which is home to a colony of bottlenose dolphins, he surely had encountered the creatures routinely. And anyone who has been around dolphins for any length of time would be very careful about dismissing anything.

Tales of dolphins playing alongside all the local boats were commonplace along the Moray Firth and all its connecting bodies of water, and over the years several swimmers had been aided and even saved by dolphins' interventions.   The entire area where the Paisleys had spent their lives is also home to several organised dolphin-watching and scientific research communities.   Folk in that whole area are inclined to respect dolphins' amazing abilities.

But the bottom line was that Jill and I just didn't have any idea what Daisy's parents knew, or how Edy might react if her daughter launched into a story that could sound like sheer fantasy.   Added to this was the presence of a woman that Edy knew only as a pleasant neighbour, not to mention a bleary-eyed, bearded journalist just off a plane from New York.

We could dither over tea and goodies only so long, and the subject of the day finally had to be raised.   There is no gentle way of easing into a conversation about humans talking to dolphins, especially when the particular human in question is sitting so peacefully at the same table.   So finally Jill took the dive.

'Daisy, you know why I asked you to meet Stephen, don't you?' she asked.   'You told me your friend Spike wanted me to introduce you to a well-known journalist, and he mentioned the possibility of an American.   I've brought along the man I trust most in the world, and naturally he's excited to hear whatever you'd like to tell us.'

You'd expect an eleven-year-old with her mother sitting across the table to be just a tiny bit hesitant about jumping directly into a discussion about previously unknown cross-species communication, but Daisy barely batted an eye before responding.

'Spike told me there were some very important things you and Mr Cameron should know,' she said promptly.

I noticed right away that there was no jaw dropping from her mum, so that was one question answered.

'He's told me that dolphins are very worried about the world. I mean, not just their world in the water, but ours, too, I think.'

Daisy paused to take a sip of her lemonade, and I interrupted only to say, 'Please call me Steve, or Stephen. Hearing you say Mr Cameron sounds kind of strange. I would like to be your friend.'

'Aye,' Daisy acknowledged cheerfully. 'That's fine.'

Then Jill nodded to her to continue with the subject in hand. Daisy took the hint without a moment's pause.

'I've been talking to Spike all this summer,' she said. 'It began one day at the Point. I heard a voice calling to me. I thought it was a man who had lost his dog, but then I could tell the sound was coming from the water. When I looked past a couple of rocks, Spike – well, I didn't know his name then – was very close to shore, and he was looking right at me. He was nodding his head.

'Some of the kids at school tell stories about dolphins, you know, and we see them swimming all the time. They whistle and make those clicking noises at us sometimes. I never thought that he was talking like a person. But then he spoke again, very clearly, and told me what a beautiful day it was, and asked if I liked coming to the shore. I looked round at some people who were having a picnic just by the lighthouse – it's only a few steps away with the tide up high – and I could see they hadn't heard anything.

'I didn't know what to think, really. Now I know that Spike understood. The next thing he said was, "You're the only one who can hear me, because I'm talking in a way that would be strange to humans. I can speak directly into your mind without the sound going through your ears."

'I didn't really know what he meant. So I asked, "How do you do that?"

'Spike whistled when I asked him the question, and he

said, "It's easy. If I want to talk and you want to listen, it's as simple as you talking to your friends. It's just that dolphins don't do it very often." '

Jill and I exchanged a glance at the term 'very often'. Was Spike saying that some dolphins have this ability, but that most don't? Or what?

Daisy was on the same wavelength, though perhaps by accident.

'I asked Spike if all dolphins could talk to us without making sounds in the air. Spike said yes, but that dolphins had decided a long, long time ago, maybe thousands of years, that it would be best if they only spoke to each other. So I asked him why. I didn't have to speak loudly because he can hear things from a long way away. Anyway, I asked why they didn't want to speak to us.

'Spike has almost always answered whatever I've asked him, but that time he just said it was a hard question, and that maybe things were going to change. I asked him how, and he didn't quite answer that, either. He said he'd like to be my friend and asked for my name. I told him it was Daisy, and he just answered that I probably should call him Spike. Well, then I wondered why he wanted me to call him something when he made it seem like it wasn't his real name, and I told him that.'

Jill was so far out of her chair that she was in danger of toppling on to the table.

'Daisy, did Spike really say he had another name?' she asked.

The girl startled us by bursting into fits of laughter. She could barely contain herself, and tears started leaking out of her eyes.

'Oh, I'm sorry,' Daisy said. 'I ken you think I've gone a bit mad. It's just that I did ask Spike if he had... you know... a real name besides what he was saying, and he asked if I wanted to know what his dolphin friends called him.'

Until then, Daisy hadn't used many common Scottish words at all, almost certainly because she was trying very hard to let us keep up. She clearly had been working on classroom English for this meeting. She'd finally broken down and said 'ken' at the same time she'd started laughing.

But she kept on with the story.

'Right away I said, "Aye, I'd love to know that," and Spike came a little higher out of the water and made this noise. Ooh, it hurts my ears just now even remembering it. It was like a whistle and a screech at the same time. After he did it, he went right back to his human-type voice and said, "Sorry, it's a little loud through the air, and too high for your ears. Did it hurt you?"

'To be truthful it did hurt for a bit, but I said no. Spike right away laughed and shook his head, and he said, "Remember I know what you're thinking, too."

'So I learned right then we can't even bother trying to fib with a dolphin. I mean, we shouldn't lie to people, either, but... you know.

'Anyway, we talked about his name another time later on, and he told me that if he was going to speak with humans he had to have a name they could say. He said he picked Spike because there are men on boats out in the firth who give the dolphins names – from marks on their fins and things like that – and he'd heard people calling him Spike. He said he thought it was a good name. I think he likes it. One other day when we were talking, he said that some scientists named another dolphin Soldier, and he was glad he didn't get that name.'

At that point I decided that I had to say something. Two questions in particular were nagging at me. The one that seemed important, at least for the moment, had to do with Daisy's mum.

'Edy,' I asked, 'how much of all this have you heard before? Do you believe – excuse me, Daisy – that your daughter really is talking to a dolphin?'

'Aye,' Edy replied instantly. 'I've no doubt of it. And I've no doubt the creature probably makes more sense than most of us. I hav' nae problem with it at all. We've just kept quiet because I don't want a bunch of people coming round and thinking Daisy's a freak, or she's telling tales or any of that. Bein' honest, I think it's grand. I wish it were me.'

My other question was for Daisy. In the big scheme of things, this was what Americans call 'the whole enchilada'.

'Daisy,' I said, 'Miss Jill phoned me just a day ago, all the way over in America, so I could come and meet you. And she said that this was Spike's idea. Is that right?'

'Aye.'

'Do you know what he wants from me?' I asked. 'Something I can do, or something I might understand? If he wants to say something to a group of humans, well, he's already met Jill, and she's been on television all over the world. We know he must trust Jill. Is there something I might be able to do or say that's important to Spike? After all, he doesn't know me, and he doesn't even know I'm in Scotland.'

Daisy smiled, the way kids can when they're trying to work out why adults sometimes can be so slow to get the picture.

'Spike knows you're here,' Daisy informed me. 'I told him just before Mum and I set off to come down here, and he seemed to be happy about it. I said that Jill loved you, that you were a famous writer from America and that we were going to meet today for apple pie.'

I probably don't need to mention that Jill rolled her

eyes when Daisy used the words 'loved' and 'famous'. 'Loved' caused her third blush of the day. The world definitely felt upside down, for lots of reasons.

'So Spike knows the story right up to the minute,' I said, as if teasing Daisy.

'Aye,' she replied, 'except that when I told him Jill was mad for this place because of the apple pie, he made a noise and told me you'd be better off having fish. I think Spike was being funny. He really can be, you know. He's even told me some jokes, but he says a lot of the ones he hears from people on boats, well...'

I went back to Topic A. 'Okay, so Spike knows I flew from America because Jill told me about you. Why me? I still don't understand. Do you know what it's all about?'

For the first time, Daisy stopped chattering. Even knowing her for barely an hour, I could tell that she now had decided to be a little careful of how she was going to respond.

'I believe Spike is worried about lots of things,' she said slowly. 'He says all dolphins are afraid of things that humans are doing. But he hasn't really explained much of it to me. He's so smart, and I'm just a child. But I am sure of one thing. I think Spike planned to explain more to Jill later. And...'

'And what?'

'I'm sure Spike wants to meet you,' she told me seriously. 'I'm pretty positive.'

'Daisy, just how positive is *pretty* positive?' I asked. 'I can't read minds like Spike can.'

Daisy gazed at me.

'So...?'

'Spike wants to meet you. Um... for certain.'

'And how would we do that?'

'Well, maybe this is just a suggestion. I'm not sayin'

anything for Spike. That wouldn't be right. But I think he wants you to come to Chanonry Point...' Daisy paused briefly and looked at her mum. 'And it's to be at high tide during the September full moon.'

I had to chuckle.

'You know, Daisy,' I said, 'that's pretty exact for somebody who doesn't really know for sure. Can you take a guess at how I'm supposed to find him?'

'Nae problem,' Daisy replied confidently. 'Spike said if you're there, he'll know you.'

I had nothing left to say, really. I'd been summoned to a chunk of land in northern Scotland by a dolphin named Spike, who could talk to an eleven-year-old girl and might...

No, I was too tired. Best not take it any further.

Jill took charge, and turned to both mother and daughter while announcing, 'The tea and treats are on me.'

Edy thanked her and added, 'Now, Jill, I make a fine pie myself. You come by when we're all back at Avoch and I'll prove it. Fact is, we could have had this conversation in our kitchen.'

'For that matter, we could have had it at Chanonry,' said Jill. 'We might as well have invited Spike and saved this young lady such a long explanation.'

Daisy giggled. 'If we'd done that, Spike would have had us eating fish. Be sure to take your own food when you visit.'

Chapter 9

En route to Avoch

Late August

We returned to the car, somehow slid out of Auchterarder, and now were back to chugging north on the A9.

A full five minutes passed before either of us spoke a word. Part of this silence had to do with the fact that Jill had dithered a bit while finding the route. She does have a few weak points, and handling cars is one of them. She claims that it comes from her days worrying about snipers and all other means of violence, but I think she's just not a very good driver, which, wisely, I've learned not to mention. And so it was quiet in our little vehicle for what seemed an unusually long time.

Finally, I decided to break the ice. 'Well, you were right. The apple pie was fantastic.'

'Told you.'

'You did. But why didn't you tell me more about the whole story before we came here? Don't you think that might have been... let's say... a little helpful, considering what's going on?'

Perhaps my question sounded like a bit of a scolding. But here was a lady who knows and trusts me, and maybe considers me someone a bit special, and she'd left out a huge piece of the tale, quite certainly on purpose.

'Oh, Stephen,' she said with a sigh, 'I just wanted to get you here as fast as I could.'

'What you're saying, really, is that you were pretty sure that my feelings for you would send me rushing off to the airport, no matter where I was. True?'

Jill laughed, softly, and sort of sweetly.

'That was part of it,' she admitted. 'I knew how much I'd missed you, missed what we had and everything. So, honestly, yes, underneath everything else I suppose I wanted to find out for certain if you still felt the same way about me.'

She took a deep breath, glanced at the road to make sure she wasn't about to rear-end a lorry, and kept talking.

'Look, my feelings about our relationship had something to do with it, but there was another very good reason for not saying anything I knew about Spike, and what seems to be going on. I wanted you to meet Daisy and hear what she had to say. I wanted you to draw your own conclusions and decide what you thought of it all.

'I was worried that you might have had a completely different mindset walking in there if I'd told you all I knew, or suspected.'

She paused for a while before continuing.

'I know quite a lot about Daisy. I've checked her out right back to birth, so I was definitely inclined to believe her. And if I'm going to be totally truthful, what I had heard myself certainly seemed to be a real, live dolphin speaking to me.

'I hope you can accept that having you walk in relatively cold was the best way to get your honest feel for things. If you agreed that it isn't some hoax or we're not all crazy or something, I was hoping you might come up with your own thoughts about what we're supposed to do next.'

Jill Gabriel doesn't lie – not to me, not to anybody. I knew that. Again she'd 'fessed up that she did have a teeny stake in finding out how much I still cared about her, and there was no denying that her logic was right about letting me meet Daisy without too many preconceptions, goofy or otherwise.

'Okay, that works,' I conceded. 'And now you know for certain that I'll probably come running from anywhere in the world if you just blow me a kiss on the phone. So what now?'

Jill thought for a moment or two. She was chewing her lower lip – the one sure sign that her mind was in overdrive.

'Stephen, before any of this goes even one step further, we have to have an agreement,' she announced.

I couldn't help smiling. I raised one eyebrow. 'No sex?' I asked.

Jill laughed out loud, stopped for a second, and then started laughing again.

'Hey,' she said at last, 'I told you already that there will be time up at Avoch, or wherever, to decide about "us", and whatever happens with that will be just fine.' She paused briefly before adding, 'Look, this agreement I mentioned isn't about our relationship or... you know.

'I want you to promise me before we say another word about the Spike thing that we'll just take it as it comes. We've got to try really hard not to judge things too fast, and definitely not start making all sorts of plans on how to handle anything until we really know what's going on. We need to understand what this dolphin might be doing.

'I'm asking you to give your word because I think we're bound to get pretty excited. I mean, I'm already there. This could be something that affects the whole world, or it could be something kind of weird and magical, that only matters to a few people and one really amazing creature.'

Now it was my turn to laugh.

'Jilly, Jilly. How in the world could I be jumping too far ahead when I don't even know what's happening? Maybe dolphins can read minds, or whatever they do, but I sure as hell can't do it.'

'Yeah, that's true,' she admitted.

'But look, sweetie, I'll make the promise. No rushing to judgment. I've been flying all night, driving up and down the bonnie braes of Scotland, and stopping for apple pie while I listen to a little girl who has regular conversations with a dolphin. How could I be forming any long-range plans?'

Jill didn't answer, but just kept breathing – wistfully, I suppose you'd describe it. She has a way of doing this that makes me want to cuddle up by a warm fire somewhere, and insist that everyone else on the planet just goes away. And she knows it, of course.

'Lie back and close your eyes, Stephen,' she instructed. 'You're at the end of one long journey, and maybe at the start of another one that could go... well, I don't know. We listened to Daisy's story together. For now, why not just lie back and rest while I get us home? I'll wake you up when we get past Inverness. Just lean back and shut your eyes. Please?'

Stretching out in a dinky Corsa is not the same as reclining on a four-poster bed in a Hawaiian resort, I should mention. I had just enough room to tilt my head and neck a foot or so. Jill reached into the back seat, produced one of the sweaters she'd bought for me, and handed it over for use as a makeshift pillow.

'Sweet dreams,' she murmured.

'I'll see dolphins in my sleep,' I replied, my voice getting kind of fuzzy.

'Soon you might be seeing them morning, noon and night,' Jill said. 'Dream of me instead.'

It turned out that Jill was right and I had been truly ready to crash, both mentally and physically. You'd think that a couple of hours all scrunched up in a car the size of a phone booth would do you more harm than good, but when Jill gave me a little nudge as she drove through Inverness, I woke up feeling almost human.

'Hiya,' she said cheerfully. 'Were we strolling on a beach, or wrapped up under a duvet in the Alps, or something sweet like that? Even if we weren't, say we were, anyhow.'

'Okay, we were.'

'Which?'

'Beach.'

'You sure that wasn't Spike wandering along with you? Positive it was me?'

'Absolutely. You two look a lot alike, but you smell nicer.'

'Ooh, you're back and chirping.'

'It's me. And where are we, young lady?'

'Not far from home. Over the Kessock Bridge, then along the edge of the firth through Munlochy and we'll be in Avoch. I've got a cottage right at the water. You'll like it. It's comfy, and it's only a few minutes up the road to Fortrose and Chanonry Point.'

Suddenly Jill stopped talking. The mention of Chanonry Point had brought it all back with a rush – Spike and his chats with young Daisy, and then the plan that I meet the dolphin during the first full moon in September, which I guessed was only ten days or so away.

We both felt a little jolt, I'm certain – no doubt considering the wild possibility that we'd be the first to report some truly startling news.

'Does all this scare you?' Jill asked.

'Maybe,' I replied. 'I'm not sure, I guess.'

By this time we had driven through the village of Munlochy, and very soon I would see Jill's home – a place I'd tried to imagine, but I never could picture it.

'Jilly,' I said, 'once I'm really awake and remember what continent I'm on and all of that, will you tell me what you've been doing since we kissed good-bye in Geneva?'

'Of course,' she replied. 'And were you also going to ask, "And with whom?" '

I kept quiet.

'You don't have to wait until tomorrow for that bit,' she told me, adding a chuckle and clearly enjoying herself. 'I haven't dated anybody, cared about anybody, slept with anybody – except a cat I had in Brazil – or even thought about getting involved with anybody since I walked away from you at that train station. Full stop.'

For all the usual stupid male ego reasons, I was thrilled, but I didn't say anything. There was nothing to add. Jill surely knew that I was pleased, for exactly those stupid reasons.

'Stephen, we may be starting an adventure that nobody could ever have even imagined,' she said. 'I don't mind admitting that one part of me is scared, but another part is hyper-excited.'

That was a startling admission from a woman who had stood in front of television cameras all over the world, while bullets pinged off houses twenty feet away and grenades blew cars to hell and gone. But I knew what she meant – there are different ways to be scared.

'That explanation probably goes for me, too,' I told her. 'It's hard not to wonder what will happen if we really do talk to this dolphin, and what he might say. It's kind of unnerving when you let it sink in. Yes, it could scare me.'

Jill turned down a little gravel road toward her cottage

near the water.

'Do you remember,' she said, 'how every night we were in Switzerland, we always held hands when we slept?'

'You have to ask?'

Jill smiled as she edged the Corsa on to a little path. I could hear the sound of the tide.

'I'd like to hold hands when we sleep tonight, too,' she whispered.

So we did.

Chapter 10

Black Isle

Late August to early September

I woke up to a world of smells – fresh-cut flowers brimming on window sills, something baking elsewhere in the house, and the lingering scent of Jill's hair on the pillowcase.

A tea kettle was whistling just outside the bedroom door. Jet-lagged or not, it didn't take more than a second for the whole pleasant mix to remind me where I'd landed after bolting across the Atlantic.

Talk about a crazy range of emotions and puzzles all wrapped up in your first few yawns on a gorgeous Scottish morning. The sun was indeed glorious, seeming to bounce off all the windows and cream-coloured walls of the cottage – at least the part I could see through the open bedroom door.

Jill must have heard me stirring, and she popped promptly into the room, obviously back from a morning run. She was wearing hot pink shorts, red and white running shoes and a grey University of New Mexico T-shirt with a growling red wolf on the front. She was also wearing a headband, which seems normal enough for a jogger, but I knew she also used it to cover up the nasty-looking scar from that bullet in Bosnia.

In fact, one of Jill's few concessions to her appearance was that, in public, she never wore her hair up, or tied back. She hated the scar, and always kept it covered. It would be easy to chalk that up to vanity, which was part of it, but I'd always thought another reason she hid the bullet crease was that she truly hated all references to the violence she'd witnessed.

At that moment, however, she was so flushed that she seemed to be glowing, as though she'd been plugged into a light socket. 'Good morning, sunshine,' she said, cheery in the morning as ever.

We had joked about that during our stay in Switzerland – how Jill seemed able to leap straight from deep slumber into a frenzy of activity approximately at the same time as your nearest rooster. On the other hand, I always woke slowly, and loved to lounge around in bed as the universe came crawling into focus.

'Hi, there,' I said, my voice sounding raspy. 'I believe you're the one who ordered a journalist from room service.'

'And delivery was quite prompt,' she replied with a grin.

She disappeared briefly, only to stroll back to the bedroom a couple of minutes later with a platter of warm buttered scones and a mug of tea.

'Cheater,' I said. 'You know exactly what I'd die for in the morning, and you were all fixed up for it.'

She smiled like a very pleased Cheshire cat, and purred, 'Well, enjoy a bit of a long lie, as the Scots call it. But don't get too comfy, because we've got things to do.'

'Things? Already? Did you have your first cup of tea with Spike?'

'No, but I did see Daisy at the baker's shop,' Jill reported. 'She was totally thrilled about meeting you, of course, but I'm not supposed to tell you so she won't be too embarrassed when we get together again. And I found out more about when you're going to meet Spike.'

Oh, really, I thought.

'Well, the full moon isn't far away,' Jill announced. 'It'll be the 5th of September, which is exactly a week from today. Kind of cuts down on the time for much thought and preparation, but I guess it shortens the anxiety span, too. I don't think I could have survived if we'd had to wait and wonder about all this for much longer.'

'One week,' I muttered. 'I suppose it's better to get on with it, whatever we're talking about.'

'There's another thing,' Jill added. 'I've got a buddy, a great old one-eyed fisherman called Hamish. He was working on his boat. It's really an old wreck, so he's always fiddling with it. I called in to see him during my run, and checked his tidal charts. I've got the times for the high tides on September fifth. You know that tides run about six and a half hours apart, right? So if there's a high tide, say, at six thirty this morning, then you'd have a low tide at one o'clock in the afternoon.

'On the day of your "appointment" there's a high tide around 3:30 in the morning, so the next one would be sometime after half past four in the afternoon. I asked Daisy if she had any notion whether the dolphin might have meant one or the other, and she said she's almost always seen him after noontime, and quite often around sunset. I asked if she'd ever asked him why, but she hadn't, so...'

'Let's stick with common sense,' I suggested. 'Besides, if Spike seriously wanted to meet me in the early hours of the morning, he's obviously not as intelligent as we suspect him to be. It's got to be the second tide. I guess I'll have another cup of tea, play golf for a few days, and then go to meet our new friend.'

'Hilarious,' Jill said in the voice she uses when she wants you to feel as if she thinks you're being a child. 'I know for a fact you'll be on the internet and in the library and heaven knows where else, researching every inch of this business over the next week.'

'You forgot personal interviews and recon work.'

'Oh, now you're making fun of me,' she complained. 'Keep that up, and you'll see how fast the tea-and-scone service comes to a halt.'

'Not that!'

'Do I seem like a woman who takes kindly to sarcasm?' she asked. 'Forget that approach unless you want to fetch your own tea tomorrow. In fact, I think we can start splitting tea duties now that you're so settled in.'

We were both chuckling by this time – just as we had pretty much every day during our time in Switzerland. There was no mistaking the ease with which we'd slid back into our comfort zone.

'And just so you know,' Jill informed me, 'Daisy's coming by for lunch. I've set up the spare bedroom as a work space, and I picked up some books for you a couple of days ago in Glasgow. I bought everything in stock on dolphin research – the usual stuff from John Lilly and Horace Dobbs, a book called "Dolphin Societies", and another one titled "Dolphin Chronicles". That last one is about an experiment several years ago with two dolphins captured in the wild, studied in captivity at a place in Florida, and then released. It's very interesting. There's also another one that you've *got* to see called "Dolphins, ETs & Angels" by a guy named Timothy Wylie.

'Apparently Wylie was a former architect who joined a religious cult of some sort, and then went on a personal mission to bond with all forms of intelligent life that humans generally don't recognise. I gather he started with dolphins, and he considers them gatekeepers to a parallel universe, or something like that. Normally I'd suggest pitching Wylie's book into the bin – I mean, he admits using all kinds of mushrooms and other wild drugs – but there are a couple of chapters about a type of dolphin communication that's really a lot like what Daisy's told us about.'

'And you, too,' I reminded her.

'Yes, and me.'

I told Jill that I'd read all of Lilly's books. He's the father of sensible dolphin study, and he began it about sixty years ago. Lilly also believed strongly in the idea of superior dolphin intelligence, and attempted several experiments aimed at trying to communicate with captive dolphins. His book – 'Communication Between Man and Dolphin' – could be considered the bible on this subject from the scientific perspective, although several more recent researchers have taken issue with some of Lilly's ideas.

And then you have a huge group of dolphin followers who won't accept any reason for the animals to be kept in captivity, and believe that all observations should be carried out in the wild.

There have been several other studies that have added to man's knowledge of dolphins' echolocation and other sonic capabilities, and a few people around the world – like Dr Dobbs here in Britain – have become international spokesmen for *Cetacea* (the genus containing dolphins and whales), and are known everywhere as champions of their welfare.

I've loved dolphins for as long as I can remember, so I'd already read most of the basic research books, but clearly I'd now have to do a cram course in less than a week, which is why Jill had been filling her house with volumes I needed to read or re-study.

'How many of these books have you read?' I asked,

genuinely curious.

'Oh, a few. And I scanned through most of them the day before yesterday when I went on the buying spree in Glasgow. You want an amateur's synopsis of the whole batch?'

'Sure.'

'Everyone agrees that dolphins have huge brains for their body size, that they have a whole range of amazing abilities like sleeping with half their brains while the other half remains conscious and lets them breathe. Everybody knows that they can communicate with each other and do sonar-type things with clicks and whistles and whatever else, and that they've always seemed to like human beings.

'They're naturally gentle, friendly and gifted. For example, dolphins can do synchronised leaps. They have ultrasonic capabilities that are beyond anything that humans could have imagined, or understood.

'That's the easy bit. Every marine biologist can recite all those things and a hundred more of the basics – like the fact that dolphins apparently can emit some kind of sound that stuns or paralyses fish, but they don't use whatever it is for anything but food. They don't even use it for defence in life-threatening situations, which is pretty amazing.

'All that is in the books we've got in the other room. Now for the grand finale...'

'And your summary from this half-century of human study of dolphins is...'

'We really don't know a damn thing.'

'Nicely put.'

'Well?'

'Jilly, it's true. Even before yesterday, when I heard Daisy's story and your confirmation of a part in it, I would have said that anything is possible. Considering how incredibly little we know about them, there is absolutely no boundary to what they might be or might know or might be able to do. None. And a week from now, we could be the ones who somehow learn a lot more of what these creatures are all about. How scary is that?'

'I told you on the way home that I feel kind of scared,' she reminded me.

'Let's leaf through those books you bought,' I suggested. 'And we can take some nice walks along the beach, and visit Chanonry Point in daylight, so I don't step off a rock and drown next week. How's that for a start?'

'Makes sense.'

'Yep, and at night you can ponder life, or whatever you've been pondering for the last few years, and at the same time maybe decide if there's an "us".'

'Is cuddling allowed while I ponder?'

'I'll risk it.'

Jill beamed her amazing thousand-watt smile, which, incidentally, could light up London on a foggy night. 'When do we start?' she asked.

'Cuddling, pondering, preparing to meet a dolphin...? Which were you asking about?'

'All of them, but you know we've got to start with Spike. For better or worse, he seems to be running this show.'

In case there was any doubt that Jill hadn't lost her touch as a reporter – and there wasn't – she already had got our research off to a flying start with a huge surprise. The woman doesn't startle me often, but she surely did by rummaging through the bedroom closet and suddenly producing a blown-up photo of our very own Spike.

Jill had contacted the people who were monitoring the Moray Firth dolphins, and it turned out that they had a few shots of the one they had named Spike.

Dolphins are notoriously difficult to photograph in the

wild, unless you have an endless supply of time and patience, and the chances of waiting for the appearance of one particular dolphin whose normal home range stretches at least a hundred miles, well…

There was one fairly decent shot of Spike from the side, with his head and torso almost fully out of the water, and another in which you couldn't see much more than his fin and tail. Jill had blown up the first of that pair, so we pinned the picture to a wall opposite the window in her work room.

There was no way to guess how the story would play out.

Chapter 11

London

Monday, September 4

Time is a funny thing.

For instance, take a single week – the time frame that was currently defining my life. For a couple on a beach holiday in the Canary Islands, a week would fly past, and they'd be on the plane ride home almost before they knew it. But for a person waiting for results of tests that could determine whether or not he had cancer – a week might seem to take forever.

These were the kind of thoughts that were flitting through my mind as I stepped off a flight from Inverness to London's Heathrow airport on the morning of the 4th of September. I had a luncheon appointment at two o'clock that afternoon with Dr Ian Edwards, a marine biologist who worked part-time with the Global Dolphin Society, and was considered to be a respected and open-minded researcher. He had been studying dolphins for more than two decades. He was deeply involved in everything from dolphin tracking projects to coordinating efforts with various dolphin rescue organisations throughout Great Britain.

My 'appointment' with Spike was now only a day

away.

We'd chosen Dr Edwards as an appropriate expert who was willing to speak with us at such short notice. There's no shortage of dolphin researchers around Avoch and the entire Moray Firth area. This is where the world's northernmost colony of Atlantic bottlenose dolphins – now estimated to be nearly two hundred – swim freely from the waters near Cromarty all the way east to the Aberdeen coast.

In the end, we had ruled out all the spotters, scientists and dolphin study groups up north. We'd decided that anyone in that part of Scotland would feel so close to their family of dolphins that it would be difficult to find someone truly knowledgeable who would also be objective. So we came up with a plan where I'd fly down to London, and see what I could learn from Dr Edwards.

I was booked on the overnight sleeper train from London's Euston Station that same night, leaving the city at ten past nine, and arriving back in Inverness at half past eight in the morning on the day that I was to meet Spike.

And now back to the concept of time, and the idea of this particular week...

Our days in Avoch and around the Black Isle had been unusual, to say the least. Jill and I felt bonded so closely now that it was almost unbearable. We took some wonderful strolls through the twin towns of Fortrose and Rosemarkie, sat for a couple of hours on two different days at Chanonry Point itself, and enjoyed each other's company at the cottage.

Spike never felt far away. How could he?

Jill had decided to tell a shortened version of our story to old Hamish the fisherman, just to gauge the reaction of an ordinary Scot to the remarkable possibilities that could be right in front of us. Hamish reacted much the same as

Edy Paisley, which confirmed our suspicion that people who had spent their lives near the open sea were much more inclined to believe what they were hearing.

When Jill had finished her tale, and had asked Hamish directly if he thought Spike really might speak to me, he didn't hesitate even for a second before answering, 'Aye, and why shouldn't he?'

Hamish had a few other thoughts as well, and promised to help us any way he could over the next few weeks.

'Lass, I'd sooner trust my life to any dolphin in the sea than most of the people I know,' he told Jill.

Meanwhile, I did most of my reading and made my telephone calls from the marvellous deck that faced the water at the back of Jill's cottage. I wondered if Spike was watching. Maybe he was checking me out – perhaps even hanging around with other dolphins and chatting about us. As Hamish had put it, why shouldn't he?

On Friday, the first day of September, Daisy had turned up at the cottage late in the afternoon with the news that she had seen Spike that same day. Not at Chanonry, surprisingly, but just off a dock near Avoch.

'He didn't joke with me as much as he usually does,' she told us. 'He was friendly, but he told me that some very important things were happening, and that some of the local dolphins weren't feeding as they normally do. He thought they'd be fine, but I think Spike just wanted me to know that he had some serious things to say. I'm just a wee kid, so maybe I didn't really understand what he was saying – not completely, anyway. But he did tell me that he hoped Stephen would come to Chanonry on Tuesday. He even asked me to tell you that. He said it twice.

'Actually, I felt a bit afraid for him. But before he left he said some things to make me laugh – like he always does – and told me to promise that I wouldn't worry. Should we be scared of something? Spike isn't going to be hurt, is he?'

Jill and I both assured her that Spike surely would be okay, that the dolphins would go on eating as they should, and that things would work out fine. Perhaps not totally reassured, Daisy only nibbled at a scone that Jill offered her, and left rather quietly shortly afterwards.

This conversation brought a hint of nerves into the cottage for a time, because it was becoming increasingly obvious that Spike's plans – whatever they were – involved considerably more than a friendly chat and a few dolphin tricks.

Jill and I spent hours, on and off over several days, wrestling with possibilities. We batted around everything we could imagine that Spike might want to say, and why he needed to communicate it.

Jill's view was that it was about human interference in the life of the Moray Firth dolphins, or maybe even all dolphins – disturbance such as underwater noise pollution from drilling, communications hook-ups, sonar experiments and so forth. Her hypothesis was that Spike had requested a print journalist from America or Britain in order to explain that these intrusions had become too dangerous, and that he wanted me to write a story about it.

I, too, had considered that this might be a possible explanation – but it didn't feel quite right. Between us, Jill and I had contacts to get a message published internationally, and Spike already had more than enough information to know that. I just wasn't sure that this could be the whole story. For one thing, if the result Spike was seeking simply entailed a powerful story explaining all those man-made problems, there was hardly the need for all the drama we were facing at the moment.

Assuming, as we knew now, that at least some of

the dolphins could actually read our minds, why not just plant the seeds of the story anonymously? From a hundred yards offshore, Spike could put whatever ideas were most important into my mind. He could do it easily. I didn't doubt that for a minute, not anymore.

And there was another thing. Spike apparently was becoming less and less reserved about speaking to humans. He'd already chatted numerous times with Daisy, he'd responded briefly to a bright, serious reporter like Jill without much hesitation, and he was keen to talk to me as well. All of this suggested that something more serious was afoot.

I found myself wondering how many others had Spike called over for a chat? For that matter, maybe hundreds of dolphins, here and elsewhere, had stopped worrying about surprised reactions and had found human partners for conversation. But we hadn't heard a word about it.

'Jill, it can't be as simple as one story, no matter how strong we try to make it,' I said. 'You don't need a rendezvous near the time of the full moon to get a reporter's attention. Remember the whale that got confused and accidentally swam up the Thames in '06? All kinds of scientists and reporters with backgrounds in marine life followed up on that story, stressing the effect of all the ocean noise that was believed to have forced the whale to lose its way, beach itself a few times, and finally die from the ordeal.

'If a dolphin, or several dolphins, decided to bring the problem to the world's attention, it would be easy for them to put the story into the minds of a few important journalists to keep it in the headlines. But nothing like that has happened. The whale story was covered on TV and in plenty of publications, obviously, but there have been dolphins beached or killed in unpleasant ways all over the world without, well...'

'Without what?' Jill enquired.

'Without an outcry from anyone, really. However you look at this, if Spike does speak to me, clearly and sensibly, then a brilliant creature like that has to know it could well be interpreted as a plea for help from all Cetaceans. That's a long jump from asking me to write one story.'

Still puzzled, Jill agreed.

On Sunday, the day before I left for the quick trip to London, Jill was particularly quiet and pensive as we sat out on the deck, sipping tea and wondering if we were about to be swamped by an afternoon storm. Scottish weather is famous for being unpredictable, and our morning sun could become rain screaming sideways within just a few minutes. Indeed, the sky was dark and brooding down over the Beauly Firth near Inverness, and it matched Jill's mood.

Finally she said, 'Stephen, do you suppose there's any chance that Spike wants to warn us about something? Maybe it's not about ocean drilling or fishing nets or anything like that. Since dolphins know so much more about the planet than we do, maybe Spike has been chosen to warn us about...'

'About what?'

'An earthquake, maybe? Perhaps it's a tsunami that's much, much bigger than the one in 2004. I don't know.'

We agreed that it was a possibility. The odd thing is that when Jill came up with the word 'warn' – seemingly out of nowhere – she was much, much closer to the truth than either of us ever could have imagined. And if we had known what kind of warning was coming, would I still have gone to Chanonry Point?

We'll never know.

Our conversation shifted to other possibilities, and

then to a very practical issue.

'Shall I come with you on Tuesday?' Jill asked. 'Spike hasn't said you have to be alone.'

Actually, I would have loved Jill to go with me, but for some reason I was absolutely sure that the dolphin wanted me by myself at Chanonry Point. I had a strong sense that Spike had somehow directed my thoughts on this, and I told Jill.

'Doesn't it strike you as odd that Spike chose not to use you as the conduit for whatever he's doing?' I asked her. 'After all, you're a famous reporter from the BBC, and your face is familiar to viewers all over the world. And he already knows you.'

Jill said nothing, and I was quiet for a while myself before continuing. 'If you press me for a wild, wild guess, I'd say maybe it has something to do with your career being almost completely involved with conflicts, with war. I could understand a dolphin not wanting that association to be in people's minds. We're talking about a species that has lived in harmony within its own environment for thirty million years.'

Jill wasn't upset. She merely nodded.

I felt badly for her just then. She'd promised me the first night we were together she'd tell me all about her activities during our years apart, and she had. Jill Gabriel had spent three years as a sweaty, routinely-ill volunteer caring for homeless and starving war victims in Africa. During one tour in Chad, she had lost sixteen pounds, and the aid organisation in charge of the project was within a day of insisting she be flown home for proper treatment. She'd also worked with the poor in Brazil, traipsing into miserable jungle regions to deliver supplies to survivors of the endless civil wars that ravage native populations all over South America.

Without question, Jill had given back value for every

penny she'd earned shipping war reports to the BBC. The once-aimless young woman who'd bullied her way into journalism simply to raise hell about unfair accusations directed at her parents had been totally transformed.

She had her faults like all the rest of us, but no one could question her motives. In fact, people who met Ms Gabriel now were likely to describe her as gentle.

Jill told me that she'd eventually wound up in northern Scotland on a whim, and she'd done it because she was thinking of writing an anti-war autobiography and wanted to be somewhere peaceful.

My heart longed to say, 'Come with me and let's meet Spike together.' My head, for whatever reason, insisted the opposite. Jill understood, which made me feel much better about the whole thing, although still a trifle guilty.

After everything that Jill had done in her post-war life, how did I deserve the 'honour' of meeting Spike? He was a brilliant creature who obviously trusted her, but for some reason, I was sure, he wanted me to go to that particular meeting by myself.

By the time I left for London on Monday morning, we'd sorted out most of what we knew – which turned out to be very little, when you think about it. Jill dropped me at Inverness airport, and suddenly it was mid-morning as I reached one of the world's great cities. As a bonus, it was sunny.

I'd arranged to meet Dr Edwards at The Twelve Pins, a combination pub-restaurant on Seven Sisters Road in the north London borough of Islington. This had been his suggestion, but a happy one for me, since The Twelve Pins is less than a quarter of a mile from the home of Arsenal Football Club, which Americans would call a soccer team. I knew the Tube route and that whole neighbourhood very well indeed.

I am, in fact, a pretty serious Arsenal fan – we call ourselves 'Gooners' – and during various trips to Britain I'd spent many fabulous afternoons at the team's famous Highbury ground. The old place had been replaced after ninety-three years by a 60,000-seat palace called Emirates Stadium. The new venue was just a few more blocks away in Ashburton Grove, so I was very pleased to travel straight from Heathrow on the express train to Paddington, and then via Tube out to Seven Sisters Road.

London's subway system is notoriously dodgy. They're always working on some line or other, and you can't really predict how long a trip will take if it involves changing at various stations. Obviously, I had to err on the side of being early for my lunch with Dr Edwards, but that was fine because the spare hour and a half gave me a chance to stroll down and admire the new stadium.

Amazingly, visiting the gleaming facility took my mind off the Spike mystery for a little while. I made the return walk to the pub past lovely old Highbury, and recalled cheering like crazy as former Arsenal superstar Thierry Henry scored a miracle goal almost directly in front of me.

Happy times, and so much simpler.

At The Twelve Pins, Dr Edwards and I arrived almost exactly at the same time, and within two minutes of being seated, I was back in the world of dolphins. Jill and I had debated just how much I should tell the biologist about Spike, and in particular about my imminent meeting. We had settled on explaining our interest as coming from Daisy's remarkable story – which I recounted almost verbatim – and I left him with the impression that I'd taken a keen interest both as journalist and as a dolphin-lover.

The scientist, who insisted that I call him Ian, had no problem with that, or even with my request to tape his comments. The Global Dolphin Society was always happy to get positive exposure, he insisted, and he could see easily enough that I was on their side.

I had decided to start by getting his thoughts on whether or not dolphins truly could read human minds, and go from there to the possibility of some sort of non-verbal communication. He had no doubt on the first issue.

'It's possible, and even likely, that they know exactly what we're thinking,' he began. 'There's a mountain of anecdotal evidence pointing to it. I could show you stacks of reports. Dolphins in every part of the world have come to help humans in distress. I've seen that myself. And they know precisely the difference between when you're playing around and when you genuinely need some help. Anyone who's regularly been swimming with dolphins – and I have – would tell you the same thing.

'As an organisation, we oppose the entire concept of putting dolphins into captivity, but there's no getting round the fact that studies done that way have proved over and over again that dolphins learn everything about their trainers far faster than the other way around. Dolphins used for these shows are supposedly taught all the tricks they do, but what actually happens is that the trainers just start the process, and the dolphins immediately understand it all – not just what the first part of the trick should be, and when they get a fish as their reward, but what's coming next.

'With all due respect to a lot of these people who mean well, the trainers and handlers are almost incidental to the process. The dolphins can, and do, train themselves. Maybe they already know what's expected because they've heard it all from other dolphins.

'As for understanding the human mind, a dolphin in captivity is usually quite friendly. Yet if a particular trainer or handler shows up one day in a bad mood, even not showing it outwardly, the dolphin might refuse to do anything. There's no doubt in my mind that they can read us like a book.'

What about Daisy's so-called conversations? I asked Ian if, as a scientist, he could consider such a thing?

'Easily,' he responded immediately.

So then I asked him if he had any knowledge of communication of the type Daisy described.

'I know of several people, myself included, who have received very, very specific thoughts or instructions from dolphins,' he replied. 'Personally, I've never had a dolphin speak to me in such straightforward language as you're describing, but that doesn't mean it can't happen. There are so-called "ambassador dolphins", who choose, or are chosen, to make very close contact with humans. I'm talking about things that go way beyond swimming around together, or letting some children stroke a dolphin's side. At places like Monkey Mia in Australia, there have been dolphins communicating with humans in some special way that has been very specific – something beyond the usual whistles and clicks.

'If you're asking me to say I'm positive that dolphins could speak to humans, either through actual speech or through something like the telepathy that you're describing with this girl, I'd have to say I can't prove it. That's what I'd tell you as a scientist, but as a person who's been around dolphins very closely more than half my life, I'd say something else.

'What you are suggesting is not that great a leap from what we already know. In fact, it's more like a logical next step.' He leaned towards me, and added, 'Always remember, what we *don't* know about dolphins and their capabilities is absolutely limitless.'

Unfortunately, Ian had another appointment that meant we had to hurry through a quick meal, using our precious time to keep on talking.

'Don't dismiss what this girl has told you,' he said, as we were getting ready to pay. 'Particularly given her general credibility, I'd say that what she's telling you is more likely to be true than not. I have to admit that I'm envious. I just wish that the dolphin had decided to speak to me.

'Sometimes I have the strangest feeling when I'm around them, as though they want to tell me something word for word, but for some reason besides the physical inability to do it, they stop short. I've felt it many times, and each time I find myself willing the dolphin to go on. I've even said "Talk to me", just hoping...'

Walking out of The Twelve Pins and preparing to head off in a different direction, Ian Edwards shook my hand and said, 'Dolphins have been heard imitating human speech since the time of Aristotle. There is considerable Greek literature about men talking to dolphins. How do we know they weren't writing about the very same type of communication that this little girl has enjoyed? Frankly, I'd bet it was. As far as I know, dolphins had no reason to be afraid of humans back then.'

And that's as far as we got.

Even without clear scientific proof, or a rousing endorsement and a string of eyewitness accounts, Dr Edwards had made a startlingly strong case for cross-species communication – actual conversation, in fact.

Once I was alone again, I laughed out loud at myself, because all I could recall at the time was that old cliché about preaching to the choir. Ian had made a very compelling and passionate argument, but I knew without a doubt that I had known his answers before I'd even asked the questions.

Heading off towards the general area of Euston Station, and eventually my train ride back up north, I remember thinking that it would be great if Dr Edwards might someday have the opportunity to converse with a dolphin as he so fervently wished to do.

I had no idea that that time was not far away at all.

Chapter 12

Fortrose

Tuesday, September 5

The only specific thing that we really wanted on the day I met Spike was good weather.

Predictably, Scotland laughed in our faces, and delivered up one of its early autumn specials. It was cold, damp and windy, with forecasts for more of the same.

'I think Spike is testing you,' Jill said, after she'd picked me up that morning at the Inverness train station. 'Surely with everything else they can do, dolphins must be able to predict the weather from sea conditions and other signs. He probably wants to see if you'll come no matter what the weather.'

'Honestly?' I replied. 'Would I give up the chance of a conversation with a dolphin just because of a bit of bad weather? You've got to be joking.'

'Okay, but ask him – for me.'

'I'll put it on the list, right alongside global warming and potential melting of the polar ice cap,' I assured her.

'Ooh, you're cranky. Tired boy. Let's get you home. A nice mug of tea, a nap, and then you can go and face your destiny. Meet a dolphin or be blown into the sea.'

Ragged as I was from tossing and turning on the train,

I had to laugh. Jill was determined to take some of the stress out of this day, because we both knew that my nerves would grow more jangled as the time drew closer.

'Hey, your friend Samantha called last night,' Jill informed me.

'Really?'

'I guess you gave her my number. She said that you'd been in touch, and she wanted to know how your project was going.'

'Where was she?'

'Barbados.'

'Perfect. I'm going to freeze to death out at Chanonry Point, and Sam's tanning on the beach.'

'I told her you were in London doing some research. She seemed to think that was pretty funny. She asked if you'd gone to an aquarium. Then she had to run. But anyway, she wished you luck and said that she was sorry you probably couldn't get any Key Lime pie in Scotland. I'm guessing that's a private joke.'

'Yep, the lady's always good for a laugh.'

'Okay. Seriously now, you need something decent to eat, and then some rest. I think we should go out to Chanonry at about half past three, in case Spike is hanging around early. I'll drop you off by that little house at the end of the golf course, and then I'll go and wait up at the golfers' car park – the one about a quarter of a mile from the beach. I'll bring some nice CDs and a headset, and just stick it out. I'll be nervous.'

'Me, I'll probably be too cold to worry,' I said.

'We'll wrap you up tight,' Jill promised. 'I've got a folding deck chair so you
don't have to stand around or be tempted to get down too close to the rocks. We can't have you too near the high tide. It really can be dangerous. Just sit in the shelter of the lighthouse wall. We'll leave the rest up to Spike.'

'It's always been up to Spike,' I reminded her.

My eyes were only half-open as we drove back to Avoch, and I was asleep about five minutes after walking through the door of the cottage. On the way home, Jill had insisted that I give her a résumé of my talk with Ian Edwards, and I had managed it.

After a little thought, Jill said, 'I'm not surprised by his reaction. I think I expected it.'

'So did I, but hearing it from him definitely made me feel a little less loony about what we're starting to take for granted. Of course, everything could still turn to nothing.'

'It won't,' Jill replied.

I tried to brace myself with that conviction several hours later, when I was finally standing at Chanonry Point, leaning against the stone memorial to the Seer. I'd had four hours of sleep, which, considering how anxious we were about the event at hand, proved just how exhausted I really had become.

Jill had woken me gently with tea and scones. Then she'd given me a special new sweater that she'd bought for the occasion, and produced a piece of white heather that Daisy had brought round for luck. Jill wedged it into the side of my wool cap.

We left the cottage at three o'clock, which seemed a bit early to me, since high tide wasn't due until after four thirty. It's only a ten-minute ride to Chanonry, but Jill had built in a little detour up to Rosemarkie, where she picked up two fresh cream scones and a couple of apple turnovers.

She put the food into a waterproof, wind-proof little picnic sack, along with a mug of tea she'd brought from home. I was beginning to feel like a small boy, being sent off to summer camp. Except that it was so cold.

It was about a quarter to four when we reached the

intersection at the end of the golf course where she was going to drop me off. Jill surprised me by producing some fresh fish. That was to be my gift for Spike.

'I can't believe this,' I said. 'He has probably eaten ten thousand fish already today.'

'He'll appreciate the gesture,' Jill assured me quite seriously. 'We've got so caught up in the intelligence and abilities of these creatures that we've forgotten that they probably have a range of emotions just as we do, like kindness and gratitude.'

What could I say to that?

So I took the folding chair, my food, the jug of tea, Spike's treat, and tumbled out of the car.

Good grief, it was windy. Never mind the cold. I could barely stand up straight. The gale seemed to be howling through the lighthouse wall.

'Hell of a day for a chat,' I mumbled.

'What?' Jill yelled from the car window. 'I can't hear you.'

I put my face into her open window, gave her a kiss and said, 'This is perfect. It's the kind of day where a mental conversation is the only kind you could have.'

Jill laughed, and kissed me back. Then she said, 'Go make history.'

She revved up her little Corsa, which struggled for purchase heading upwind, and gradually disappeared back up the long Ness Road.

So there I was, alone. Or possibly not...

It was getting close to four o'clock. A wild and crashing high tide was banging its way on to the Point, and I went off to find the spot along the wall that we'd picked out so carefully earlier in the week. Of course in the sideways wind and a thick mist, it was pretty much impossible to re-create a walk made during low tide on a sunny day.

I gave up on the folding chair, and wedged it between two huge rocks that form part of the craggy shoreline where the boiling sea meets the wall. I decided I could hold on to everything else. I wandered around – or more precisely, staggered around – through the wind looking for a decent vantage point. But it was hopeless. Everything was waves and foam. In these conditions, I began to think that I would hardly have noticed Spike if he had come ashore and sat down beside me.

If this dolphin wanted to meet me, he was going to have to be the one doing the navigation work. With that decision made, I celebrated with a few quick hits of tea. Then I scrunched myself up against the lighthouse outer wall to sit it out...

And waited.

That's when the bird-watcher came strolling down the road, appearing out of the fog, and making my heart do a quick thump. What on earth would bring anyone else out here on an afternoon like this?

I found out soon enough. He was looking for a pink-throated something-or-other, and sometimes they appeared on gloomy days at Chanonry. Fortunately he departed after only a brief conversation.

So I was alone again, and there was nothing to do but wait some more.

Nothing dramatic happened, except that my attempt to nibble one of the turnovers was ruined by the wind. I seemed to be at the end of nowhere, and I was wondering if I might be the nuttiest person in Scotland or anywhere else.

Near enough to five o'clock, the wind dropped noticeably. I was truly thankful for that. The tide was high, with the water only a few yards from my boots.

I decided to stretch my legs, walk the short distance over to the memorial, and ask the infamous Coinneach

Odhar for some spiritual assistance. Surely the ghost of a man boiled in tar would hang around for an occasional request.

Coinneach didn't answer me, but somebody else did...

'Hello, my friend,' said a voice that was startlingly clear and distinct.

I thought I had prepared myself for this moment. But ask yourself: Could anyone react calmly to a greeting in perfect English from a 1,300-pound sea mammal, in the midst of a full-blown storm?

An unbelievable shiver shot up my spine, and it had nothing to do with the weather.

When I responded, it seemed to me as though my voice surely would be lost in the wind, and I had only a vague idea in which direction to face.

'Are you Spike?' I yelled out in the general direction of Fort George.

Jill and I had considered about a hundred different greetings, and had hit upon three or four we really liked, but of course I had forgotten them all. In fact, I nearly forgot where I was.

'Yes,' said the voice, again so nice and crystal clear, despite the wind and rain.

Jill and I had also laughed a lot in our debate about whether Spike might have a Scottish accent. We decided that he almost surely would, since it would be the voices of Scots he'd heard most of his life. But what I was hearing – or not hearing, but 'processing' – seemed to be devoid of any accent, and sounded a little like something from mid-western America.

On reflection, I suppose it could be that Spike's 'voice' would sound American to me, since I'd come from that country. Maybe he could communicate in whatever language or accent might be comfortable to the listener, because I'm sure Daisy said that he sounded Scottish to her.

'Are you nervous?' Spike asked.

'Yes, I guess I am,' I replied. 'I've... I've never spoken to someone who could read my mind.'

'Jill can,' Spike answered, following those 'words' with a very real and audible cackle that cut right through the wind. 'Please don't worry. Most people's thoughts are a bundle of confusion anyway. Millions of them per second, if you're interested. Yes, we can know what you're thinking if it's necessary, but dolphins usually only bother to do this when there is something important to learn. With our friend Daisy, she is able to say aloud what needs to be said. It's simpler to have contact with someone like that.'

I was concentrating so hard that I almost didn't notice that Spike had gone quiet. Maybe he was waiting for me to speak, but I was still in such a state of confusion that all the carefully thought-out questions that Jill and I rehearsed had disappeared from my mind.

'Can you forecast the weather?' I asked, suddenly remembering that Jill had insisted on that simple question.

'Yes, very easily,' Spike replied. 'And please tell Jill that she was right. I chose today for our meeting because of this weather. I'm sorry that you felt uncomfortable in the cold, but for this first time, I believe it was necessary that there was no one else here. I wasn't expecting the bird-watcher. Persistent people, aren't they? I was afraid he might have stayed around a while longer, but I knew you were getting colder, so I sent him a suggestion that perhaps it was time to go home and sit by a fire.'

'Well, obviously the wind doesn't affect how well you hear me,' I said, 'and however you are communicating to me, I understand you perfectly.'

Spike spoke again. 'I know that you and Jill have spent a lot of time wondering why I need to speak to you, and what could be so important that I would arrange a meeting like this. I will explain why, and then I'm going to ask you to help us to do something very serious, very important – but also very good.'

'Okay,' I answered. 'Tell me.'

I heard nothing more from Spike for what seemed to be quite a long time. Waves banged into the sea wall, and somewhere in the distance a foghorn boomed out into the mist.

Finally I heard him say, 'Save the world.'

Spike's statement made me think of how many times we have used that phrase – on bumper stickers, as a part of jokes, or on the chest of Greenpeace T-shirts. You hear it so often that it has almost become background noise.

But the incredible clarity with which Spike had spoken the words suddenly changed their entire impact. There is no way I can reproduce those three words as the dolphin had conveyed them. However, I did know one thing with absolute certainty. I've never felt more positive about anything.

Spike meant what he had said, and he meant it in its absolute literal sense.

'Now I'll begin the story,' he said.

Chapter 13

Chanonry Point

Tuesday afternoon

It had begun.

'You are not comfortable,' Spike said.

I really didn't have a quick answer to that. Was he talking about the fact that I'd wrapped my arms across my chest to keep warm? Or was he asking if I was anxious, or even frightened?

'No matter how much you prepare,' the dolphin said, 'or how intelligent you are, you might well feel disturbed at the idea of speaking to me – a creature who speaks directly to your mind without an audible voice. This is entirely unfamiliar to you, but any anxiety you might feel will soon disappear.

'You are a man of many years, with ideas and habits programmed into you, so it will take a little while to become used to speaking like this. Your young friend Daisy felt at ease in just a few minutes, because she had no reason not to accept things just as they are. Please don't worry, and remember that there is no need for you to try to do anything differently. Our communication will happen as it happens.

'Adapting to new things is part of the natural way.

You will hear me talk about the natural way quite often while we speak, and again at other times. You will come to understand it with very little effort.'

Again, there was nothing for me to add.

Spike then said, 'When you hear me speaking about time – minutes, hours, days, weeks – it is of course time in the human sense. Dolphins do not conceive of time in this way. For us, the natural way is simpler. The past *was*, the present *is*, and the future is only the future.

'Forgive me. Your discomfort is also because you are cold. I will change that now, because you need to feel relaxed. We are going to talk about some very important things, and you need to be at ease.'

At that moment, I felt a tingling throughout my body. It was not an unpleasant sensation, and it lasted only a few seconds. But suddenly, everything seemed to change. The chill was gone, and the wind seemed to have dropped to a light breeze. It was almost as if I had been transported instantly to a beach in California on a pleasant afternoon.

'I have altered your mind slightly, but it is temporary,' Spike explained. 'Your brain is now telling your body that the ambient temperature is seventy-two degrees Fahrenheit. I also reduced your hearing so that the sound of the wind won't distract you. Please remember that I am not here to hurt you, and that the changes I have made will vanish, leaving no permanent effect.'

For obvious reasons, I trusted the dolphin completely. I'm certainly not a genius, but even a hint of common sense suggested that Spike possessed powers and abilities that were utterly beyond our understanding. And so I felt no fear at all.

'You are right to realise that there is a great difference in our capabilities,' Spike said. 'I know that you believe in the concept of higher thought and perception, and what might lie beyond it, and that you accept that you can never understand everything about it. I can tell you that we know that higher worlds exist. To make dolphin intelligence simpler to understand, think of it as accepting something far beyond anything that humans can comprehend – at least at this time in the universe.

'There is also the same impossible, unknowable difference between what we dolphins and whales can understand, and what is known in eternal wisdom. We have always understood that. Just as I am suggesting that you think of the great gulf between man and dolphins in this way, that is how we accept the concept of higher worlds. That is part of the natural way.'

I was feeling quite a bit more comfortable, and I had lost much of the shock and anxiety that comes in the process of communicating with a creature so far beyond normal comprehension. And of course, I was warm and relaxed, as Spike had said I would be. At last I began to feel sure enough of myself in this remarkable situation to speak up.

'Do you want to tell me the reason why you've brought me here, and its connection to our world?' I asked. 'The idea of saving the world, as you put it, is very dramatic – at least to a human.'

Spike waited for a considerable time before he answered. Under the circumstances, it would be almost ridiculous for me to hazard a guess as to what he might be thinking, but my instinct suggested that he was making a decision.

At last he replied. 'You know that I can understand your thoughts. Reading a human being's feelings and reactions, and interpreting what his mind might produce from them, is quite a simple thing for dolphins. It is not perfect, like reading a book word for word might be for a man. But if we choose, we can understand what you are thinking in a way that can be quite specific.

'You might be surprised, however, to know that it is not something we do very often. We would much prefer to live as we always have, in the natural way, as dolphins do, without having to be concerned with other creatures. We do not judge any of them, including man.

'No being is either good or bad. We avoid sharks, and sometimes must defend ourselves against them because their nature is to consider us as prey, in the same way that we must consider fish. All creatures live, feed, and preserve their own species.

'The concept of "reading" human beings, and anticipating what they might do, isn't something new to us. I cannot tell you how long it has been the case, because it started before I was alive, but dolphins' relationship with man has been based on something like brotherhood for thousands of what you would call years.

'The conversation we are having now may seem a remarkable event to you, but when dolphins and humans were more equal in each other's eyes, this type of communication was common. Dolphins didn't consider it special, nor did the men of that time.'

For some reason, Spike's revelation about human communication with other species in another era didn't surprise me. For one thing, it reminded me of what Dr Edwards had said. And why wouldn't creatures sharing the same planet talk to each other, in whatever way was available to them?

Just for a second, I remembered old Hamish saying: 'Aye, and why shouldn't they?'

So what had happened to shift the balance, and to convince dolphins that they were better off avoiding us – in order to go on living and loving and enjoying their great world in the sea?

'How did it change?' I asked, even though I was aware that Spike knew precisely what had crossed my mind.

'I cannot answer that,' the dolphin answered. 'It is a very sad thing, and it is the reason I asked you to come here. Even now, with our species and the entire planet in serious danger, dolphins all feel a deep, deep sadness about being cut off from humans. Every day, all over the world, dolphins are swimming or playing with human beings. Sometimes their thoughts come very close together, so it would be easy for us to speak. But we do not. It has been a long time since we spoke freely.

'There are exceptions. For instance, dolphins will talk to the minds of children, or to humans with illnesses or mental difficulties. Not only are these people more naturally open to us, but also they are people who are unlikely to be believed if they claimed to be speaking with us. We used to enjoy the chance to talk to all humans. After all, we are close cousins to humans in some ways, living side by side.

'The reason that things changed was our need to continue our own way of life. Man has grown and changed. I do not mean that as a compliment. Man has developed his technologies and his growing sense of power over all things.

'At some point, man's ego raced ahead of his ability to remain living in the natural way. You have come to believe that you rule the Earth and all things in it, and that you have the right to control the plants, the minerals, the skies, the seas, and even other creatures who mean you no harm. Most are not even necessary as food for your survival.

'I can communicate these things to you because you are open. You can see now that we have abilities beyond you, including the wisdom to know which of these abilities and how much of our intellect we should use in the natural way.'

The mist had lightened a bit, but even though I'd heard Spike's mental messages clearly, I still hadn't seen anything of him, apart from a glimpse or two of a fin between waves. But all at once, he rose up out of the water, with half his body extended, not twenty feet away from me.

Oh, wow!

I knew from our research that the bottlenose dolphins around northern Scotland were the largest in the world, but I wasn't quite prepared for the sight of Spike, and certainly not such a sudden appearance. He looked huge.

Spike was clearly visible and seemed almost close enough to touch. 'Stephen, I want you to understand about the natural way,' he said. 'Hold up one of your fingers. Just one.'

I poked up my right index finger. Within a second or so, I felt a little jolt and the finger went numb, as though it had been hit with a super-sized shot of Novocaine.

'Don't worry,' Spike assured me, 'your finger is paralysed now, but this will pass in just a minute. I wanted you to feel the effect of a sound that we can produce. It could have been thousands of times stronger – enough to stun you, or stop your heart instantly. We use that kind of sound wave on fish. We must eat in order to live. There are other possible uses, as well, which we will talk about later.'

Once more there was a pause.

Other possibilities? Talk later?

Spike spoke again. 'We do not use this power to defend ourselves. A dolphin attacked by a shark would fight, but he would not use that stunning sound, even for survival. I think that now you are able to tell me why.'

'It's not the natural way of things,' I guessed. 'But how are decisions like that made? Why would a dolphin fight a shark by other means, when it might cost him his life? And despite all your echolocation abilities, dolphins are still caught in nets. They're herded into bays in places like Japan and clubbed to death. Why?'

'Nature requires a balance,' Spike replied, 'and that balance needs a certain understanding from creatures with higher intelligence levels or overwhelming means to harm others. Humans might call this our morality.

'We've never had to make a decision about this. Our way of being is the natural way. Dolphins will not upset the balance of our planet. We have a wonderful life in the sea, my friend. And so I would not want to be caught unaware and lose a fight with a shark. Like you, I would prefer not to die. But sometimes such things will happen, because the world was created in a beautiful balance and no creature has the right to alter that balance out of selfishness.

'In any case, what would be the point? Dolphins understand these things better than man, but we do not claim to possess the highest form of intelligence. We are certain we do not.

'As for the matter of using our skills for survival in all cases, or even as aggressors, it would not be right. Maybe if we swam from one end of the Earth to the other, and used every skill and power available to us, we could kill millions of creatures – including sharks. But that is not natural. The world was not meant to be full of dolphins and without any sharks. That has never been right.

'So we live in the natural way – allowing the world to stay in balance, not disrupting it. Dolphins never have to think about that – we understood and accepted it long before man was on Earth.'

Spike's explanation seemed so incredibly simple and profound that I was left standing there with nothing to say.

The dolphin continued. 'I know that what I am asking

you to understand is an enormous challenge for you, but you truly need to grasp it. You must take it into your head as I'm communicating it, and also into your heart. If you can do this, then I will be able to explain why we're here at this place, and how I would like you to help me.'

'I'm only human,' I murmured, straight away realising that I'd used a really worn-out cliché. In this case, though, it carried a sense of literal truth. I was most certainly just a man, and what could I possibly do to change any of the things Spike was describing?

'At this moment, it's humans we need,' Spike explained. We've reached a place where humans must help or we are in very, very great danger.'

What did he want me to do? Did he want me to write a story?

'You are quite gifted with words,' Spike answered, reading my thoughts. 'I am sure you would do justice to a great book if we spent months or maybe years together. You could write about magical things, wonderful things that men don't yet know. Unfortunately, we do not have time for that. Not now.

'Stephen, please understand that all dolphins have put off this moment for as long as possible, because we hoped that things would change. We hoped that man would evolve.

'Your wonderful scientist Albert Einstein once said his greatest fear was that man's ability to create new technologies would accelerate faster than his sense of how to use them. I'm afraid that time has come. Man is racing out of his own control. For the sake of all of us, this situation must stop now.

'I know that you and Jill have talked about the whale which died almost in the middle of London. It happened because his brain became overloaded with so much unfamiliar noise in the sea that none of his natural faculties would function. All that destructive noise was man-made.

'The natural way of things has been disregarded almost completely. Man has laid cables on the ocean floors, filled the skies with satellite signals, burned down forests – destroying millions of animals – and almost certainly will change the Earth's temperature to a level so dangerous that none of us will survive. And while all that is going on, men are building weapons and more weapons to kill each other. In the process, they are likely to destroy this planet, which is our home.

'Only people can stop this. They must. Governments and businesses can help, but we need millions of ordinary people to join together and insist that the madness must end now.'

The wind at Chanonry had dropped. Everything had become completely still. The weather was clear. Had Spike's adjustments to my inner heating system worn off? Was this now a pleasant September evening?

I could only state the obvious. 'Tell me what to do.'

'I want to speak to a group of people,' Spike said. 'It should be a small group – perhaps six. To communicate that way is the most effective. For me to be certain of being understood, it is safest to speak with no more than two people at a time. I will leave this part up to you and Jill, but if you arrange for six people to be present, I would talk to them two at a time, repeating the same message to each pair.

'From what dolphins have learned about humans, we know there are some intuitive things that men and women can grasp about each other. We are gathering knowledge from all over the world every second of every day right now, and we have amassed a great body of it. But now I need to trust you and Jill about something that requires uniquely human instinct.

'You must try to find the right people. Half of the group should be journalists representing networks or outlets that reach most of the world, and the others should be scientists who are specialists in marine life and general environmental conditions.

'I want to give the reporters a message to broadcast, and I need the scientists to provide whatever information is necessary to back up my statements, because so many questions will be asked.

'I know that there will be many objections. And there will be loud cries from people whose personal interests are in conflict with we know to be basic truths. It will not be easy.'

Spike went on to explain that he was certain that Friday would be sunny and clear in this part of northern Scotland, and therefore we should arrange the meeting for that day.

'I haven't given you much time. I realise that, but we cannot wait. I know that a pleasant day will bring more visitors to Chanonry Point, but our group will be small. I hope that you can arrange the meeting for a little after 6 a.m. Most visitors will not be out by then. It is early for humans, and it is an hour after high tide, which will be best for us.

'At that hour, there should be enough light for any television people to see me. There will only be the voices of the reporters and scientists, who will have already spoken to me. Each of them will receive an identical message from me – in the same manner that I'm speaking to you now. There may be sceptics in the group, so I might need to speak with a person individually quite briefly, explaining some things about themselves and their lives to prove how much we know...'

Spike whistled briefly before continuing. 'Whatever it takes. And after they understand what I've said, they must go on television and into every newspaper, over every satellite communication, in every language. They have to repeat this message precisely. It is critical to the safety of every living creature.'

I tried briefly to envisage how Spike's once-in-a-lifetime press conference might actually play out in real life. I wondered exactly who ought to attend, and whether Jill and I could get them to the Black Isle at the appointed time. And would the right people buy into this?

'Do you believe that this will work?' I asked.

'It must, which is why the message will contain two parts.'

'Two?'

'Yes. First I am going to give them all a shorter but perhaps more powerful version of what I've told you today, and I will tell them that the future of the world's population depends on how successful they are. But there is second message, and it hurts me even to mention it.

'For some time, we considered leaving out this second part. But that would not have been fair to mankind, which must know the full truth of what we are saying. So there must be a warning, as well.

'Unfortunately, even though there are millions of good people who would do the right thing simply because it's right, there are also others – many with power and influence – whose egos and long-established personal sense of entitlement won't allow them to see the dangers I've explained. And there will be some who understand the dangers, but who simply don't care.

'Don't underestimate the self-interest in these kinds of people. It's something that dolphins, even studying humans as relentlessly as we have done in recent times, truly do not understand completely – the concept of evil, or greed for its own sake. That kind of reasoning is beyond the most intelligent dolphin who ever lived.

'Sadly, we know that this mentality does exist in the human species. Somehow, humans have developed the capacity for useless violence, and this will have to be taken into account in my statements, because after I speak on Friday, we are not likely get another chance quite like this one.'

I suspected that I knew what was coming next, so I just looked out towards Inverness and waited for Spike to continue. What he was about to say couldn't be easy.

'You understand that for dolphins to choose a path that would defy the natural way would require something almost unthinkable. But we have almost reached that point. You know by now, Stephen, that our powers – some that have never even been used – are far past all human understanding. There is only one reason which would force us to suppress all our natural instincts and beliefs, and that is for the survival of the planet.

'Your thinking just a moment ago was correct. I am going to present a careful, reasoned message to the world – backed up by science, and by common sense. However, I am going to strengthen that message with a warning.

'It won't be complicated. I am going to say that all dolphins are telling mankind to stop, to halt their incredible damage to the planet, and to move toward the natural way of life that benefits us all.

'If mankind in general, or a group with powerful business interests or even a fully armed government will not stop, we will stop them ourselves.'

Spike fell silent, no doubt to let me absorb the overwhelming impact of his statement. I tried to imagine how such a 'threat' might strike the reporters – and especially the scientists, who would have started the day completely enthralled by the prospect of communication with a dolphin.

The picture was scary.

Spike continued. 'I will tell them that we understand man's technologies and his weapons. These have been devised by what to us is still relatively limited intelligence. Even Man's most powerful weapons are primitive to us. Yet certainly my statement will lead to their asking what a few thousand dolphins, spread across vast oceans, possibly could do if challenged by mankind.

'They may wonder what would happen if people decided to exterminate us. For example, they might think of using nuclear weapons in bays where dolphins feed – attempting to get rid of us, instead of thinking about the greater good. Yet they have no idea what they would face, and I do not want them to know too much about what would take place if they treat us as enemies. But I can give them a hint of it, because I do want to make them cautious, or even afraid.

'Remember that little tingle you experienced on your finger? I will demonstrate that power on Friday – and tell everyone that, if we choose, the stunning effect could be a thousand times greater, or more. I will ask each person to imagine all vessels at sea being incapacitated because the crews are paralysed or dead. I will ask them to imagine an immeasurable blizzard of sound knocking out satellites and disrupting computers, thus stopping all human communications.

'They must understand that there are dolphins all over the world, and that we have the ability to freeze minds, change opinions, and cause havoc or confusion in all human interaction. In fact, we can halt human activity completely.

'As terrible as it sounds, and as painful as it would be for thousands of gentle dolphins to carry out, we could put any human life or all man's civilisation in jeopardy – and we could do it all in a matter of minutes.

'So you see, for the purpose of Earth's continued

existence, dolphins would abandon the natural way. Despite man's certainty that he rules every inch of the planet, he is wrong.

'It would be a terrible thing for us to use such force, but if it became necessary, we would have no choice but to do so. We would employ all our abilities to prevent the destruction of our planet.

'In such a case, those humans who threaten the existence of life itself would have no chance, no defence. None at all.'

We both fell silent and remained so for a while. At that moment, Chanonry seemed a beautiful place, with a few rays of light still hanging over the western hills. Waves continued to slap at the rocks, throwing a light spray across the Point. Our conversation had been wonderful yet terrifying, and Spike knew that this was in my mind.

Then he said, 'Think about how to arrange the meeting I've requested, and we will talk again tomorrow. Bring Jill with you. Come back here around the same time.

'I should say that you and Jill would be protected from any dolphin action against mankind, as much as it is possible. You will be kept safe. And since you arrived early today and got so cold, I have a little gift for you.'

With no warning at all, I felt my right arm and shoulder tingle briefly, and then my left.

'Hey, my shoulders… '

'I knew you were going to visit a dolphin park in Florida to get some help for those shoulders,' Spike informed me. 'Please don't worry if you're thinking that I disapprove. There are logical reasons for having some captive dolphins. In fact, they learn a whole lot more about humans than the other way around. They're our front line. They have fun with their shows, too. And most of the trainers and park owners are kind. Not all, but enough of them.'

There was a silence, and then I heard the words: 'Do not lose heart.'

After that, quite suddenly, Spike was gone.

Chapter 14

Avoch

Tuesday, late afternoon

During the ten-minute walk from the lighthouse back up Ness Road to the golf course parking area, I wrestled with my thoughts. How would I explain it all to Jill? How would I re-create the wonder of Spike, as he described the assignment he'd asked us to take on? And how would I remain straight and honest about the possibility of some frightening consequences?

I was expecting Jill to jump out of the car and grab me by the shoulders, shouting, 'What happened? What happened?'

Instead, she sat motionless on the driver's side, staring at me, wide-eyed, and simply nodded for me to hop in. When I did, she leaned over and gave me a very quick kiss, and then let out a long sigh.

'You're not going to believe this,' I said, sort of breathlessly.

'I will,' Jill answered promptly. 'I heard it all.'

Now *that* statement was as stunning as anything Spike had said. Well, almost. I'm sure that I must have looked at her like a crazy person, because if somebody had asked me to take a thousand guesses at Jill's first sentence upon my return, what she had actually said wouldn't even have made the list.

I am rarely speechless, but this turn of events brought me close to it. Jill simply sat still and looked directly at me, her expression unfathomable, waiting for me to say something.

'What do you mean?' I tried. 'Are, uh, you saying...'

'Yes.'

'Yes... what?'

'Yes, I heard your whole conversation with Spike. I have no idea at all how he arranged it, but I've given up trying to understand these things anymore. Maybe dolphins created the world. Maybe we're all going right out of our minds. If you weren't here experiencing the same things, I think I'd be tempted to go down south to Brighton or someplace and jump off the end of a pier.

'Do you know what I was wondering while you were walking back up here? Figuring out which media people and scientists to summon on Friday, maybe? Or perhaps working out how to explain the situation to them without giving away too much, but still making sure we get their best people? Or trying to imagine what could happen if governments or whoever won't listen?

'Actually, I wasn't thinking about any of those things. I was trying to figure out how Spike managed to pipe the entire conversation into my head so that your voice, yelling into the wind, was exactly the same volume and had the same precise clarity as his.

'Stephen, we could be quite batty before this is over.'

I laughed. 'I know the answer.'

'You do?'

'Spike temporarily adjusted your hearing to the pitch of my voice so that the noise from the wind dropped out of what you were hearing.'

'How do you know that?' Jill asked, raising her voice

a little.

'I think he just told me,' I replied.

'Oh.'

And that's what the dolphin had done. Of course he'd anticipated that, with our human limitations, Jill and I wouldn't understand how he'd managed to include her in the conversation from a quarter of a mile away in a high wind. Then I heard his voice, quiet and patient, explaining the procedure. And finally, he told me to take care of Jill, and said a quick good-bye.

This, to me, entirely new method of cross-species communication was slightly unnerving, but after what I'd seen and heard, I was almost beyond surprise.

Jill, meanwhile, had recovered her usual composure – a state which wavers only very, very rarely. This is a woman, after all, who had routinely spoken into a microphone, completely still in front of a video camera, while bombs exploded and people were shot dead in front of her.

'Okay,' she said, 'at least now we know what it's all about. I've got to admit that some of what I heard was pretty scary, but it was also just so... fascinating. I can't think of another way of describing it.

'But look, this wasn't a one-time visit. Obviously we've got work to do, and with stakes so high that they're really beyond our imagination.'

'Jill, don't you feel kind of, well, exposed – dealing with creatures who obviously can get into our minds and our lives at will?'

'Oh, no,' she replied. 'I thought about that for a while, even when I was listening to you and Spike, and I realised something really important about everything that's happening. See, right now we're hearing these stories about dolphins reading minds and planting ideas, and it all seems like a strange piece of science fiction.

'But remember, we've only ended up like this because they've come to a crisis point. That's why all their abilities – no, *some* of their abilities – have been heightened or sharpened or whatever. Right now they need to know what certain humans are thinking. And like in our case today, they'll do something that might seem out of character if it's necessary.

'Just think, Stephen, you're a great reporter, with maybe the best memory I've ever known. But you don't have a tape of everything Spike said. Everything's in your head, but even with your memory, it would have been impossible to recount the whole conversation when you told me about it, wouldn't it?'

I agreed.

'So Spike made sure I heard everything. Doing it that way saved us a lot of time. And now there's a lot we have to do. Oh, and Stephen...'

'Hmmm?'

'I've got to admit that I was excited – yes, and flattered – that Spike included me. He trusts me to be a partner in this, and that feels good.'

'Surely you couldn't have doubted that he trusted you?'

'Well... no,' Jill answered slowly. 'But Stephen, sometimes I miss a few things. And although I know I've always sounded sure of myself, like going on camera in a war zone, once in a while I could actually hear my knees knocking together. And remember in Switzerland, you found out I'm truly terrified of mice. Me, the girl who saw all that bloodshed. I'm not quite the rock I wanted the world to see.

'You must know that. Of course you do, because we've laughed about it in the past. But I've got some of that "woman" thing going, too. I suppose it's the kind of thing that makes women check their hair in the mirror.

Most women appreciate compliments.'

'So our special friend Spike understands this on top of everything else?' I replied.

'Oh, he does,' Jill agreed. 'He definitely does.'

It made me feel much more comfortable to hear that Jill's voice was back to normal.

'Hey,' I said, 'now that we've got everything sorted out, can we go home and get something to eat? Since you were tuned in on things all the way along from the comfort of the car, you know I haven't had a bite to eat.

'Um, not to mention that we have a hush-hush press and scientific gathering to arrange – something that's supposed to reach the whole world. Jill, we've got to pull it off. Maybe you're used to the international stage, but this is even bigger than that. I need a little time to get my head round it.

'Factoring in travel time for whoever's involved, and the fact that we're up here near the top of the world, we actually have only hours at our disposal rather than days. True?'

'Gotcha,' Jill replied, revving up her never-say-die Corsa for the trip back to Avoch.

We didn't talk much on the short ride back to the cottage, but I did ask her to explain a little bit more of how she felt about the dolphins' use of their ability to understand human minds.

She was happy to oblige. 'I think they're basically happy creatures, who would consider any other being friendly unless it's obviously not true, like in the case of sharks. And I assume that the type of enjoyment they take from each other and their environment would mean that it was mostly uninteresting to read thoughts, let alone from a bunch of ordinary humans.

'For example, they wouldn't get any pleasure or satisfaction from listening to fishermen gabbling about town whores, or reading someone's mind to see if he really likes his job or if he's thinking about quitting. I mean, only humans would waste time watching reality shows, seeing people doing nothing of any value. On the basis of our television choices alone, I'd guess we're probably the most boring species on Earth.'

I chuckled. 'I suppose if you judged humanity solely from its devotion to current TV programming, that would be a fair assessment.'

The more we thought about it, the more it felt like much of mankind must be in an emotionally wrecked state. We found the notion almost amusing. Maybe it was our way of coping with the awesome events we'd witnessed, and the staggering task we'd been given. But just to put one foot in front of the other, we each had to keep a sense of balance – not to mention our sense of humour.

'So the bottom line,' Jill concluded, 'is that I don't think dolphins pay a hoot of particular attention to us unless there's something important enough to make contact necessary.'

'And obviously the current situation qualifies.'

'Obviously.'

'What you're suggesting is that dolphins have been taking some time gathering what we would call tactical intelligence,' I said. 'Just in case...'

'Yep.'

'Well, if that's the situation, and I think it sounds right, then I hope they're good at it, because to tell you the truth, I don't trust the human mindset any more than dolphins do. Seriously, can you picture the United Nations convening a special session or setting up an emergency committee on the basis of one dolphin's press conference?'

'Only if it's pretty spectacular.'

'Then we'd better get to work.'

Which we did – but only after I finally got something to eat.

Jill had never claimed to be a decent cook, and my own skills are ridiculously basic. If we hadn't brought in meals, or eaten out during that winter in Switzerland, the authorities would have found two frozen corpses in the spring thaw.

But somewhere along the way, Jill had tried to go domestic. And she'd reached what she called the 'sandwich, pasta and casserole' level quite nicely. So that evening, she seemed proud to produce a spaghetti-and-something dish with quite a flourish. There was no five-star restaurant in her future, though, except maybe as a customer.

After dinner, it was back to business.

We decided first of all that Jill would contact the media people. She was much closer to the big decision-makers at places like the BBC and CNN. Neither of us really knew much about the scientific side of it, except from reading the names of famous people who were strung out all over the world.

I did suggest Dr Edwards from London, since I'd already met him, and I knew that he'd be inclined to believe what we were going to tell him. Ultimately, Jill came up with the plan that I'd get in touch with Ian, first thing in the morning. We'd invite him to Friday morning's gathering, but I'd also ask him to put forward names of a few others whose reputation was strong enough to carry weight under questioning, and who could get to northern Scotland in time.

We agreed not to contact anyone that same evening. We were still too much in a state of… something… after our encounter with Spike, and I could imagine conversations that might sound a bit too close to hysteria.

Jill decided she would ring Daisy to let her know that I'd met Spike, since the girl probably would have been on pins and needles all day. Jill could assure her that it had been a wonderful visit, and that I had even agreed to help Spike to pass along a message to people about the environment.

This was all true. Not exactly the full picture, but true enough for the moment.

Once that call was made, Daisy seemed satisfied, which gave Jill the idea that she ought to drop round sometime in the next day or so to share the whole story with Hamish. She knew that the old fisherman would be waiting for news, and that he would understand whatever she told him. Furthermore, he might have some sound practical advice.

We also decided that the general plan would be to ask invitees to arrive in the Inverness area on Thursday night. Jill would rent a suitable vehicle – a people-carrier, actually – and pick them up very early on Friday. I would be waiting at Chanonry Point on Friday morning and would act as a guide.

Spike had made it very clear that neither Jill nor I could be part of his conversations with these guests. He didn't want our pictures taken, either, and we were supposed to claim that we knew nothing about the content of the dolphin's message.

Besides hauling guests around, Spike saw our jobs as using our credibility to get the right people to Chanonry Point, and convincing them that, yes, a dolphin could and would speak to them under certain controlled circumstances.

Spike was betting, and we concurred, that journalists and scientists would be so curious about all this fuss that they wouldn't dare miss it. Even a hoax or failure of some type would be a decent enough story for the media folk.

Jill was still so well known that her presence alone would draw the networks. But Jill and a talking dolphin? That would be a cinch. We started with this premise, never varied from it, and were proved entirely correct.

Later, we gave up our planning for the night, and just sat out on the deck with a nice view of the lights glimmering over towards Fort George.

'How do you feel?' Jill asked.

'Exhausted, when I think about everything that's happened,' I replied. 'But I get totally energised when I remember what it's all about. I really do.'

'Still scared?'

'Sure, a little,' I answered. Stating the obvious, I added, 'This isn't, like, everyday stuff.'

'We just have to try our best, I suppose,' Jill said.

'Exactly. The best thing is to concentrate on what a special gift we've been given, and respect and value it.' I looked straight into her eyes. 'Jill, we'll share it, and keep it precious. Let's just stick with that.

'As for possible unpleasant consequences, well, Spike obviously is right about the fact that this planet is heading for something terrible whether the dolphins intervene or not. There's no use worrying about the part of it we can't even influence, let alone control. We've got to trust Spike's plan. Look, people might worry about getting hit by a bus if they cross the road. But it's no use living your life without stepping into the street. We've got to keep going, believing that good will come from whatever we manage to do.

'One thing we should take away from everything we've learned is what totally harmonious lives the dolphins lead. Why wouldn't any sane person want to imitate that as much as possible in our own environment?

'Remember that the dolphins only disrupted the way they live because they're convinced that we're getting too close to a total catastrophe. They're acting on that now, but I suspect they're still playing, eating, mating and enjoying themselves. And they're too smart to worry about that one-in-a-million chance they'll get hit by a bus – or in their case, come across that one clever shark.'

'There *are* no clever sharks,' Jill said, smiling at her own wit.

'There are no clever buses, either.'

We both laughed at our bit of silliness, and after the pressure of the day, it felt nice. Tomorrow would be phone calls and check lists, and our social call on Spike in the afternoon. But now, somehow, we both felt prepared.

We held hands and watched the lights across the firth.

'Haste ye back, Spike,' Jill murmured, using an old Scottish expression.

A few minutes later, we rose to go inside and get some proper rest at last. Jill began padding around in the living room, rearranging notebooks and reference materials, and then dropping some things off in the study.

'Ooh!' she exclaimed, quite suddenly.

I jumped round the corner with a what-the-hell look on my face, and found Jill smiling broadly.

She was gushing. 'Spike answered.' She continued to grin like a kid. 'Remember that I said: "Haste ye back?"'

'Sure. What did our friend have to say, then?'

Jill was still smiling as she replied: 'Aye! Spike said: "Aye"!'

Chapter 15

Fortrose

Wednesday

It was a busy morning.

First I sent an e-mail to my pal Samantha in Houston, suggesting that she keep an eye on the news, particularly international items, over the next few days. She knew I was working on a story that had something to do with dolphins, and I couldn't help chuckling at what she might see if things went according to plan.

As for our strategies, it became pretty obvious that Jill would have to be the point person for all our media contacts. She knew exactly who to reach at all the major networks that broadcast around the world, and even better, they knew *her*.

Not only that, but no one could question Jill's credibility. Even though it had been several years since she'd been on the air with one major story after another, she'd kept in touch with the top brass at the BBC. She told me that she sent Joe Bass, one of her key news editors, postcards from time to time – solely to assure him that she hadn't gone missing in Tibet, or anything else truly disastrous.

Jill was never very specific about where she was,

because she was sure that she didn't want to work at this point in her life, and she knew that they'd come calling as soon as they had something they felt really needed the Jill Gabriel touch. On one occasion Jill had even phoned Bass, telling him that she was in Canada when, in fact, she was bunkered in some wretched little village in the wilds of Brazil. But she had a great relationship with Bass – who'd been promoted since her departure – and she was sure that he'd jump when she rang up to talk about Spike.

Jill had two worries. One was that Bass might beg her to handle the assignment herself, which, to be truthful, she probably would have liked, and the other was that she needed somehow to convince him to send someone with a solid background in marine and environmental issues.

And I had a niggling worry which didn't make me feel particularly proud. 'Hey, Jill, I hate to sound like a typical, you know, jealous guy in the middle of making history,' I said, 'but this guy Bass...'

Jill faked being insulted, and then winked.

'He was just a great boss,' she responded. 'But it's nice to know you can still sound like a boy who wants to carry my books home from school. Look, Joe is super-sharp, he was always fair, and he'll believe me because we always shot straight with each other. You'll see.'

And of course, at Jill's end the whole thing went like a charm. Jill caught Bass on his mobile, gave him just enough of the really good stuff that he was practically jumping through the phone, and made him promise to have somebody in Inverness by midday on Thursday for an early Friday meeting with a 'special' dolphin.

She even trusted Bass enough to give him her number at the cottage and my mobile number, but made him promise to keep everything between himself and one good reporter. Bass told her the man he'd send was Andy Hendricks, and without running down all of Hendricks' qualifications, Jill assured me that he was solid as a rock, very knowledgeable, and the kind of guy who would report the story objectively. That was everything we needed from him.

We were even luckier at CNN, which technically had been Jill's competition for years. On her first try at reaching the worldwide network's London bureau, she found a woman called Barbara Williamson – someone she knew well on a personal level rather than from working stories in various battle zones. Better still, Barbara was CNN's environmental specialist for Britain and Europe.

In a fifteen-minute call, Jill had wrapped up an arrangement, and had told Barbara to ring her from Inverness on Thursday. Jill said later that she felt so good about the conversation that she had almost invited Barbara to dinner at the cottage. Fortunately, at the last second she realised that we'd be emotionally charged and logistically challenged by then, and needed to be on our own. In addition, it would be rather unethical to let Barbara hear in advance anything about what was going to happen the next morning.

We needed an international wire service that would complement the media coverage, and decided on Reuters, which was respected everywhere, and had enough specialists that the odds on someone turning up who was a financial analyst were tiny enough to be ignored.

Jill didn't know anyone well enough at Reuters to take the direct route, but fortunately her name still rang enough bells that she was able to make contact with a science reporter named Randall Carter. It turned out that Carter had been a fan of Jill's work during her blood-and-guts days, so he was happy to chat. He was naturally intrigued when she explained about her involvement in this amazing saga of the Moray Firth dolphins. Carter said he'd check with his boss and get back to her, which he did, within the hour.

Jill had been very careful to tell the media people just enough to interest them in the story, although merely her own presence on the scene might well have been sufficient. She also tried to be breezy enough in the explanation of a Friday 'briefing' to dissuade anyone from picking up too strong a scent and showing up three hours after the phone call.

The key to everything was getting everyone to the Black Isle at the right time, and Jill managed it perfectly. She didn't go anywhere near disclosing the fact that these people would be listening to a live dolphin in a meeting that would make history, and instead told them all that she was collaborating with an American journalist on a book project, and that they'd come across some truly remarkable events involving dolphins in and around the Moray Firth.

She added that she would be out of the area until Thursday afternoon, hoping to slam the door on any ideas of a surprise visit. We also posted a huge sign over the kitchen phone that read: 'Only Stephen answers!'

Jill felt relatively sure that no one suspected the truth. But after all, it was reporters we were talking about, and they weren't exactly rookies. These folks were *extremely* experienced at sniffing things out. You can't hide Jill Gabriel very easily, and I thought that even starting from scratch, a first-rate journalist could have been on her doorstep in half a day. But Jill seemed completely confident that the gang from London would wait two days and show up on command, so I simply decided to trust her.

Besides, what choice did we have?

Meanwhile, I was assigned to find the scientists we needed, which was a little more complicated than it sounded, because neither of us really knew enough about who was in the general area. And how close would they need to be, anyway? Somewhere in Europe?

As planned, I rang my new friend Ian Edwards at the Global Dolphin Society. Luckily I caught him in his office, which, considering his normal schedule, was almost like stumbling over a needle in a haystack. Unlike the reporters, however, Ian deserved the truth – and I shared it.

I explained what had happened since our lunch in London, and apologised about not having mentioned Spike at the time. I told him we still had not been sure that the meeting really would take place, and gave my view that telling the story earlier could have caused considerable embarrassment.

Ian was so excited by my story, which he never doubted for a minute, that he shushed my apologies immediately, and simply asked when and where we wanted to meet him. After that was done, I informed him that Spike had requested three media representatives and three experts from the scientific community. So I asked Ian if he could help by recommending a couple of fellow travellers for this adventure.

I knew that by requesting this, I was putting a very good man on the spot. Anyone Ian mentioned, and who could make it to Chanonry, was likely to become part of a worldwide hubbub. This meant that Ian had to choose very carefully from dozens of capable friends and colleagues who would have traded their entire careers for this opportunity. Fortunately he understood the dilemma, and came up with a remarkably sound idea based mostly on geography.

'It would help immensely if you could get someone from America,' he reasoned. 'The reaction in the United States to what's happening here will be a crucial one. That's not a problem where the press are concerned, as they'll spread the word everywhere in an instant, but eventually you'll be needing an American expert with unquestioned credentials – for testifying to Congress, chairing committees, and handling interviews in the States.

'There are several people who would be suitable, but there is one I'd recommend in particular – Dr Gordon Jamison. He's a field biologist who has his own base called Keys Research Group in Florida. He's also a lecturer at several major universities. And by a happy chance, he's in Edinburgh this week, participating in a workshop on the dangers of North Sea oil drilling to various types of marine life.

'Gordon is a very well-known, well-respected scientist, and has corresponded over the years with virtually everyone who matters in this field – from John Lilly to Horace Dobbs and certainly the researchers at Monkey Mia and elsewhere. His name isn't so widely known in lay circles, perhaps because he's never been particularly interested in writing books for the general public. He's a good man, and a totally objective observer – even more so than myself, I have to say. I know him fairly well. I was invited to the same event in Edinburgh this week, but just couldn't get away. I happen to have his mobile number here on my desk.'

I tried to hold back my eagerness, but probably didn't do a very good job of it.

'Would you mind ringing him?' I asked, with barely disguised urgency. 'Or I can do it myself if you feel this puts you in an awkward position?'

'No, no, I'll call,' Ian assured me. 'And I'm sure he'll find a way to get up there. Actually, he's been trying to talk me into going to Edinburgh for dinner on Thursday, if you can believe it. How much should I tell him?'

Now we were getting to really difficult issues. But I

made the big decision and jumped in with both feet.

'Say whatever you think is necessary to put him at Chanonry Point,' I said. 'I trust your judgment. If you have a problem, or Dr Jamison somehow is tied up, let me know as soon as you can, and we'll go another way.'

I gave him the numbers of Jill's house phone and my own mobile, and was ready to ring off when Ian added, 'I might have an idea about your third scientist.'

Needless to say, I was ready to hear it.

'I'm a great admirer of a retired professor and researcher from the University of Aberdeen called Mo MacDonald. It's Dr Morris MacDonald, actually, but he gets quite huffy if you don't call him Mo. I understand your logic in thinking of experts from somewhere further away, but his presence would cover you all the way round. You'd have working researchers based in London and Florida, plus a tremendously well-respected local man.

'And I can tell you that Mo MacDonald will be believed. He's infuriated influential people on every side of every issue surrounding *Cetacea* over the years. He's the kind of person who won't go along with the crowd just because everyone gets excited. Mo sticks to facts, and proof that will stand scrutiny. He's top-notch in a situation like this. If a dolphin does communicate and the message is important, you need witnesses like Mo, whose integrity is impeccable.'

I asked Ian if he thought Dr MacDonald could be contacted quickly. As he was no longer officially working with the university, he could be anywhere in the world, perhaps snorkelling among a few hundred of his finned friends.

'I'm not sure on that one,' Ian admitted. 'I've got phone numbers for him, and for people who sometimes know where he's gone, even when he'd rather not be bothered. Honestly, I don't know. But Steve, this could be the most important breakthrough we've ever known in cross-species communication.

'I'll start trying to track him down straight away. I'll call you later today, and if Mo has gone off to Fiji or something, we'll see if we can think of someone else. I've got to call Gordon in Edinburgh right now in any event, and he might know where to find Mo. It's a pretty close-knit group of researchers. I'll get back to you as quickly as I can.'

I told him that his plan was perfect, and added that I was really looking forward to seeing him again later in the week.

While I was tied up on the phone, Daisy had been round, and Jill had taken her out on to the deck for a chat. Daisy had to be told a bit of what was happening, but in a way that wouldn't scare her half to death. And she'd get less of a fright when newsreaders on the BBC started talking about dolphins predicting serious danger for the planet.

Daisy had left by the time Jill and I met for tea and an update around two o'clock. By that time, Ian had called back with the brilliant news that he'd found both of his friends Gordon Jamison and Mo MacDonald. In fact they'd been sitting in a pub together in Edinburgh, discussing the workshop.

'It sounded as if they were just relaxing over a meal,' Ian said. 'You needn't ever worry about those two. They'll be sharp as tacks on the day. Mo taught for forty-six years, and people in Aberdeen swear that he never missed a single class. I believe them.'

Predictably, I was close to euphoric at that piece of news.

Apparently, all three of the scientists had already booked rooms for Thursday night at the Travelodge in Inverness, and would contact us when they reached town.

Perfect.

Surprisingly, though, I found Jill in a somewhat grumpy mood when we finally sat down to compare what, by then, looked like a string of successes. We had our six people with the ideal qualifications, and it certainly seemed that they would all be in the right place at the right time.

Jill was annoyed with herself. 'I can't believe I screwed this up!' she muttered, banging her tea mug on our little deck table in irritation. 'How many years did I do stand-up reporting? How well do I know that business?'

She wasn't expecting an answer, and didn't wait for one.

'I forgot all about the camera and sound people.' She took a breath and then moaned. 'Stephen, how in the hell could I forget about the crews? Andy and Barbara are going to need footage of Spike. They probably think they'll have dramatic audio, too, so that's going to be an unwelcome surprise. The only audio they'll be able to send is stand-up stuff, along with some quotes about what they've heard from Spike. And I suppose they can interview one or two of the scientists.'

'Or us,' I reminded her, adding that Spike had told us to try avoiding publicity. 'It would be logical. If you were doing this story, wouldn't you want to know how these two characters came upon a talking dolphin and managed to gather a press conference?'

'Absolutely,' she agreed. 'The only thing is that the actual content of what Spike will be saying truly should turn out to be more newsworthy than the fact that he's speaking at all. From what we've heard already and the threat itself – which is all you can call it – I'd say that maybe the story will be so big that you and I might actually slip under the radar.'

I thought about that. The best I could do was a 'maybe.'

'Listen,' I said, 'we're due to go and have another chat with Spike soon. Let's just ask him about our own role in all of this, and what he'd like us to do with the camera and sound people.

After all, it's his show.'

'Yep,' Jill agreed, still fuming over her failure to remember the drill for basic TV field reporting. 'Plus, he's obviously a lot smarter than we are.'

I had no dispute with that. Of all the things still left to ponder at that point, the level of Spike's intelligence certainly wasn't one of them.

'He's had an answer for everything we've asked, or even thought of asking,' I pointed out. 'We've already got lists all over the house. Just scribble down another one called: "Questions for Spike." '

As it turned out, our chat with Spike led to resolutions to our logistical puzzles. For example, he left it in our hands to make any final decisions about the use of the camera and sound people. And in the end we decided to say nothing more to reporters about that subject.

After all, Spike knew that there would be no audio of him in any case.

In the end, the main theme of our second meeting with Spike turned out to be somewhat the opposite of what we had expected. Certainly, he was friendly and informative – happily sharing things that were common knowledge to dolphins but a total mystery to us. For one thing, he told us that the local dolphin population was amused by all the longstanding fuss over the so-called Loch Ness monster.

Although Jill had listened in to everything the day before, she was now having a real interactive exchange with Spike, and such fragments of information thrilled her.

Me, too, for that matter. Spike clearly enjoyed having a conversation about something other than the fate of the world, and what unhappiness might be required to safeguard it. He gave us plenty of background about the 'monster', while Jill listened like a schoolgirl. Spike reported that, yes, dinosaur-like creatures did live in the loch, and that this had occurred well into what historians might call the modern era.

Spike told us that the depth of Loch Ness, and an unusual food supply that came from the outside water flow, had allowed these huge animals to flourish for centuries longer than their land-based cousins. Eventually, though, the food had dwindled, and Nessie's kind no longer could satisfy their giant appetites. Spike confirmed that the appearance of some of these creatures was similar to the current sightings in the loch.

Spike also surprised us with a very serious question for Jill, and it was obvious that this was about something which troubled him.

'You worked in television and went to places where there were wars,' he began.

Jill actually looked a little sheepish.

Spike, though, seemed genuinely puzzled. 'I know that you have rejected that kind of work, and since then you have spent years helping victims of conflict, but I would like to know if you, or Stephen, can tell me what it is that causes human beings to seek out wars.

'Dolphins have always lived alongside creatures of all kinds. Because of the need to eat, some live and some die, but we know nothing of a compulsion to kill just for the sake of killing. We understand enough about man's wars to hear the justifications – religious differences, the need for land, desire for power or money – but no dolphin is capable of grasping the sense in any of it.

'There is no such thing as 'war' – the way humans

practise it – anywhere else in the universe, on land or in the sea, so why does it happen?'

Neither of us had any plausible explanation, of course. There is none.

'Perhaps we haven't evolved long enough to shed our fear of losing authority, or losing control of land, or whatever,' Jill suggested. 'I don't know what else it could be. My last day doing broadcasts was from a war zone in Bosnia, and a little boy was shot right in front of my eyes. He was buying an apple from a man with a cart just outside the door of his house. After that happened, I put down the microphone, told the camera crew to pack up, and flew back to London.

'All that time, I'd told myself I was just doing a job, being a messenger. But now I believe that the media actually help to keep wars going by contributing to the escalation of anger in the people of these countries. I've seen situations where eventually they don't even know what they are fighting about, yet they become more and more savage out of frustration. It's complete madness.'

Spike glided slowly up toward the rocks, and with the tide so high, he was almost right at our feet.

'You are good people,' he said. 'What will happen when I talk to all these humans will cause arguments and confusion and perhaps some ugliness, because not all leaders and other powerful people are going to react to the message properly, or understand it in the way we intend.

'I am afraid for the world. It is only because of this fear that dolphins are about to do something that is so alien to us. I am also afraid for you and those close to you, because I am placing you personally in some danger.

'I cannot rule the oceans and the land and the skies, so like any other creature, I cannot promise you will not come to harm. But I can tell you that every dolphin alive will attempt to protect you. There are others like you, far away, who may take similar risks, and we will do our best to look after them, also.

'I do not want you to live in constant fear. That is not part of the natural way. But I do want to say now, before any of these things begin, that if you feel yourselves to be in serious danger, please move as close to open sea as you can. We will always know where you are, and we can protect you. We hope to be able to manage it no matter what happens, but it will be easier if you are closer to us.'

Neither of us could say anything to that. Hearing such a powerful and yet kind animal, a spirit so much more intelligent and closer to everything that matters in the world, speak with such sincerity... well, it was a profound experience.

There's no other way to describe it.

Jill bent down, and letting the water slosh over her boots, she touched Spike on the top of his head – technically, his melon.

'I think you're in more danger than we are,' she told him. 'There seems to be so little we can do, but we'll help however we can.'

Spike slid sideways just a few feet and let me stroke him for a minute, as well. We knew that he was reading our minds. Each of us felt fear for the other two, and yet there was no turning back, because the stakes were too high.

'It could end wonderfully,' Spike reminded us. 'So many people are acting like disturbed children. And now such people must put down some of the deadly toys that could be used to destroy all of us. We can make this happen, and after that you must promise you will come and swim with us. And then, even back on land, you will start to live the natural way.

'I have many things to do now, and will be gone until our day. Other dolphins will be all around you. They will talk to you if you need to speak to them at any time. So I will say good-bye for tonight, and I will see you soon. After that the world will not be the same.'

Chapter 16

Fortrose

Friday morning

Was I nervous?

Yes.

Did Jill seem nervous?

No. But of course, she wasn't a stranger to television cameras, press briefings, and all of that – not to mention life-and-death situations. She'd even been through routines like this while snipers pinged shots off her jeep a few yards away.

I suppose I was expecting something approaching chaos on the big day, but Jill was magic. She claimed to be a bundle of nerves, but it didn't show – although she did burn our toast. On the other hand, I had no problem making tea.

Everyone we hoped to have in the area had phoned the previous day. Each time the phone rang, we laughed because of the giant sign instructing me to answer in case someone was searching for Jill.

The scientists were at the Inverness Travelodge, and so was Randall Carter. We wondered about that, because although Jill didn't know Carter personally, she knew of his reputation in the field, and thought that he very well might recognise one or more of the scientists if he bumped into them. Fortunately, that didn't happen.

The BBC gang had taken rooms at Lucille's Bed and Breakfast near the centre of Inverness, while Barbara Williamson and her crew landed at the only hotel in Fortrose, and weren't aware of how close they were to Jill's house, or to the site of the planned 'conference'.

We hadn't told any of our guests exactly where on the Black Isle we intended to gather, because we didn't want camera crews wandering around Chanonry on Thursday, looking for good vantage points and generally nosing around.

Maybe Spike was right. It would go well.

Our logistics were very simple, as the layout of the area dictated. There was really only one place for Spike to meet anyone – at the spot next to the lighthouse, just as you go round the corner from the east to the north side of the ness. There's a long straight wall there, which meant that we could keep everyone else back out of sight of the dolphin until we walked them down to the water. There's a long open space along the beach, not far from the end, but it had no road access, and we thought that any early morning wanderers could be sent in other directions by the dolphins if it came to that.

My job was to act as guide. After Jill delivered the entire group to the parking area nearest the beach in her rented vehicle, I would meet them and escort each pair round the corner of the wall and down to the water's edge as Spike had requested. Jill's people-carrier was roomy and comfortable, and a good enough place for others to wait their turn.

There wasn't a lot of room to move around at the water's edge, but the space would give everyone a place from which to see Spike from about fifteen to twenty feet away, which he had insisted was adequate for his purpose of meeting two people at a time. When we had last seen Spike, I'd wanted to ask him how he could do that, but time had slipped past.

Jill and I decided that we should pair each journalist with a scientist. For one thing, the competitive reporters might not behave calmly if we made them do anything side by side, and for another, if there was a critical question to be asked about something Spike didn't cover, it was likely to come from a scientist. So each of the media members, in effect, would have a scientific 'advisor' right at his, or her, elbow during their meetings with Spike.

Neither Jill nor I would be present for any of the conversations. Spike had insisted on that from the beginning, to lessen the focus on us. Jill and I would be portrayed as helpers or messengers, as if we weren't privy to the information Spike had to share. Yet we doubted that these sharp journalists would believe that for very long.

Jill was to stay with the vehicle, providing tea, coffee and breakfast pastries to anyone who might be interested, and keeping an eye on those who decided to take a walk outside the vehicle. In practice, we weren't worried that anyone would sneak down to the water during someone else's interview, because they simply couldn't get there. That was one of the advantages of arranging these meetings at high tide.

Each pair of guests would pick a number out of Jill's cap, and in this way they would visit Spike in whatever order their luck dictated. Because Spike had planned exactly what he would say, and he would repeat it precisely to each pair, the number would merely dictate who heard it first.

We joked about the possibility that Spike – of all the creatures in the world – might become like one of us, and forget exactly what he wanted to say. Yet we knew that realistically he could do it perfectly a thousand times, even while half his brain was sleeping...

The plan was that I would begin by warning everyone that the rocks were slippery. Then I'd lead the first pair past the lighthouse, along the wall and down to the spit of land at the end. I wasn't to say another word, except to tell them that they would be in that place for exactly thirty minutes, and that the dolphin in front of them wished to communicate in a way he would explain to them.

In the case of the television crews, one camera person could come along and wedge himself or herself against the lighthouse wall.

It was now just after 6 a.m., the time Spike had specified, and the day was unfolding in exactly the kind of weather he had predicted. Naturally. It was cold, but not unbearably so, not for northern Scotland in the autumn. Our guests all seemed pleased with the bright, clear morning, and chatted about it more than this kind of group normally would – most likely to ease some cases of nerves.

Although they didn't have any idea what the true scope of this 'meeting' would turn out to be – except for Ian Edwards, who was almost completely quiet – both the reporters and scientists had already sensed instinctively that they hadn't been summoned to some kind of stunt.

I felt as though I could reach out and 'touch' the anxiety that was running through almost everyone who had turned up. They weren't saying much and they could not possibly have guessed at the magnitude of what was awaiting them, but it was obvious there was a thrill of excitement vibrating through the entire group.

Then, at last, it was time.

I remembered Jill's anger at herself for forgetting the camera and audio people, but that didn't really come into play at 'show time'. As it turned out, the BBC had sent a separate technician, and he was politely told that he couldn't go any further than the lighthouse, but that he could tape whatever he saw and record wave sounds for background if he chose to do that.

Barbara Williamson of CNN brought a camera-sound man, as well, and he was told the same rules.

Andy Hendricks and his camera man joined Gordon Jamison in the first pair. By the time we were ready to set off, there was such a palpable sense of tension amongst the whole crowd that it raised the hair on my arms.

But things seemed to go smoothly.

I took Andy and Gordon down to the water, and after half an hour, I led them back up to the van. Both were absolutely silent – almost scarily so. I wondered what would happen once they started talking to each other, but I didn't have time to wait around and find out.

Randall Carter and Mo MacDonald were the second pair – no camera man this time – and again, everything seemed remarkably in order. When I was bringing that second pair back up to Jill's vehicle, they were whispering, clearly trying to make sure that I didn't hear what was being said. I wondered which part of the story they were trying to hide from me.

I chuckled to myself.

Finally, it was time for the last pair – Barbara Williamson and my friend Ian. Barbara was smiling as we walked across the sand and turned past the wall. Ian has that effect on everyone, even with all the tension.

I learned later that throughout the three sets of meetings, Spike emitted no audible sounds other than soft, steady breathing for each half-hour. This meant that the two networks obtained pretty much the same thing – video of a large male dolphin in the early morning sunlight, with audio that consisted of nothing but waves lapping against the rocks and an occasional question from either a reporter or scientist who seemed to be speaking to an open body of water.

I was truly curious to know Ian's reaction, and when I was walking alongside him on our trip back to the car park, he turned and said quietly, 'Steve, I don't know whether to feel honoured or just plain terrified.'

Obviously I knew what had made Ian's blood run cold – or at least I thought I did.

At any rate, I asked, 'Would you rather not have been part of this? It should certainly make some type of history.'

Ian seemed too preoccupied to discuss much more, but finally he said, 'No, I understand why you wanted these particular people here. It had to be this way.'

He paused briefly while he checked to make sure that Barbara was off talking to her camera man, and then he said in a low voice, 'Spike really is fantastic, isn't he? Do you ever get used to talking to him, or are you always in the same kind of awe?'

'Always,' I replied. 'But you do get used to the type of communication – hearing things in your mind, and not through your ears. I really hope you get a chance to talk to him again, because he's a wonderful creature. He can be quite playful, but today, well, for this occasion he had to think of the whole world.'

Ian nodded, but said nothing, since we were just reaching the main group.

Between each of my treks back and forth, I tended to stick with Jill near the waiting group, and we made a conscious effort to give the journalists and scientists whatever space they cared to take. The only time that the six chosen interviewers would be together with someone who hadn't participated would be when Jill took them back to their lodgings.

Spike had directed us to refuse any requests to hang around Chanonry Point immediately after the meetings. However, the area is partly public land, so anyone would be free to return later. As for questions that any of the six might care to ask Jill or me, Spike said we should use our own judgment about what we answered. After all, we knew roughly what they had heard.

Or at least, we believed we did. Yet we discovered soon enough that we were quite wrong about that.

Right on time, the 'event' was finished and Jill rounded up everyone. It seemed that there was a kind of a buzz going on, rather than real conversation. She herded the crowd into the people-carrier for the ride back to their lodgings. She told me later that, except for a couple of pleasant, meaningless exchanges, no one had said anything during that journey.

The instructions Spike gave me to follow after the interviews had ended were simple. I was supposed to take Jill's car and return to the cottage. Spike didn't want me to come back down near the water, because he assumed that one or more of the journalists might well return fairly soon. And he was right, because Barbara Williamson, along with her camera man, had been dropped off in Fortrose and begun to march straight back along Ness Road to Chanonry Point.

I have to admit that's exactly what I would have done under such circumstances. As it turned out, her efforts were futile, however, because by the time she reached the Point, Spike had disappeared.

Over the previous couple of days, Jill and I had talked about what the hours would be like between these early morning meetings and when the first news broke.

Would it be a news flash – perhaps on the radio? Both the BBC and the CNN seemed certain to rush something online, and then follow it with dramatic packages on television. Both have 24-hour news operations, so we assumed we'd know something soon.

The only puzzle that nagged at Jill – as a former TV correspondent – was Spike's choice of timing. She reminded me that the news of whatever happened at Chanonry Point would break in the wee hours of the morning in the United States. In the news business, and especially in a situation where the power and influence of the US almost certainly would be put in the spotlight, the rule of thumb is to get stories on the air during prime time in New York and Washington.

I tried not to think about those details. A creature far more intelligent than either of us was making the decisions, which seemed like a pretty good plan all around.

And what about when the news finally hit?

We were sure we'd be nervous and excited. We tried to guess how each journalist would report what they'd heard, and if any or all of the media people had interviewed the scientists, but we just didn't know, and we weren't sure how long we'd have to wait. At least we'd be able to judge the accuracy of each agency's content, because we knew exactly what they'd heard.

Or so we thought.

Chapter 17

Avoch

Friday noontime

Jill saw it first, and she let out such a gasp that I heard it from the kitchen.

'Stephen!' she shouted.

Then she started to holler again, but I'd already rushed to the doorway to see what had happened.

'Look at this!' she yelled, pointing frantically at her computer. 'Look!'

Between Jill's shouting, and her sudden grip on my arm, it was tough to see exactly what she wanted me to read. Finally I found enough balance to see the screen over her shoulder.

It was a news bulletin timed at 11:42 a.m., and it must have been posted by Randall Carter or, the more I thought about it, someone else in his office. Randall would still be around Inverness, or perhaps on a flight back south, so whatever he contributed would have to be sent to London, checked and edited, then released on Reuters' international wire.

I tried to scan through it, but at first I couldn't quite take it in. So I started again and read every word...

LONDON (Reuters) – Officials from the U.S. Department of Defense refused to comment Friday on reports that one of their newest nuclear submarines, USS Eel, is lying helpless and without communications several hundred feet under the North Sea.

However, a group of journalists and scientists conducted a televised press briefing at 11:15 a.m. (UK time) from Inverness, Scotland, at which all six insisted they had been given information about the current plight of the submarine by a dolphin in the nearby Moray Firth earlier that morning.

Representatives of Reuters, the British Broadcasting Corporation and CNN all participated in the teleconference, along with three scientists whose expertise relates to various practices within the field of marine biology.

All six people claimed that they were taken in pairs to the edge of the firth at a place called Chanonry Point, where they received clear and precise communications from the dolphin – despite the fact that witnesses standing just a few feet away heard no audible conversation.

'It has been a long-held belief that dolphins have sound and telepathy capabilities beyond human imagination, and today we've been given a demonstration that even our wildest speculation may have undershot the mark,' said Dr Gordon Jamison, a marine biologist who has been studying dolphins for more than two decades from his base at the Keys Research Group outside Key Largo, Florida.

Jamison, Dr Ian Edwards of the Global Dolphin Society,

155

and retired University of Aberdeen professor Dr Morris MacDonald saw the dolphin – who is called Spike by researchers around the Moray Firth area – individually during half-hour periods, and each of the scientists was accompanied by a member of the media.

Randall Carter of Reuters, who contributed to this report, was present along with Andrew Hendricks of the BBC and Barbara Williamson of CNN.

The media representatives were invited to this morning's gathering by Jill Gabriel, former BBC correspondent who has spent several years as an aid worker and was believed to be working on an autobiography while living in Brazil. Five of the people present at the event know Gabriel by sight, and told Reuters they were positive she was the person who drove them to Chanonry Point.

'Jill said she had an amazing story to share about some dolphins doing remarkable things in the Moray Firth region,' Carter said.

'She told me that if we came up on Friday, we would get some spectacular pictures and hear a story that would "rock the world",' according to Williamson, a member of CNN's London bureau.

'I heard this dolphin as clearly as listening to a good car radio,' Williamson said. 'He told us his name was Spike. He explained briefly that dolphins always have been able to communicate with man, but had stopped doing so centuries ago because humans had become a dangerous species. His most critical point – and all six of us agree we heard the same words – was that mankind's technology now has outraced his maturity to the point that the entire

planet is in danger.

'The dolphin listed several man-made causes for global problems in general, and marine life in particular, and said he and all dolphins were asking man to step back and re-think his entire way of life, that it was necessary for survival.'

Dr Edwards of the London-based Global Dolphin Society, which oversees whale and dolphin research and several rescue organisations throughout Great Britain, indicated that the dolphin, Spike, appealed for peace and common sense, but made it clear that dolphins have powers and abilities '... far, far beyond human comprehension – and that they will step in to save the planet if they must.'

Edwards said the dolphin told all six people with whom he communicated that as an example of how quickly the world's species Cetacea could cripple human activity, they had incapacitated an American submarine called the USS Eel while it was submerged in the North Sea at a depth of 400 feet.

'This dolphin called Spike told us all – and each of us agrees on the wording – that the event happened at 0500, British time, and that there were no injuries or loss of life on the submarine. However, the ship was without power or communication as a result of a six-second ultrasonic blast more powerful than has ever been used by man, but less than 10 percent of the force available to dolphins. He said that as matter of morality dolphins always have refrained from using this "weapon" – except in very low doses to stun fish for food.

'Spike told us that all efforts to contact the submarine

would be useless, and dolphins would prevent any attempt to reach the ship. However, each of us heard him say that the submarine would be restored to full power and allowed to go on its way without harm at 1300 hours today.'

If the facts allegedly passed from the dolphin to bystanders are correct, the Eel would be incapacitated for exactly eight hours and released with no damage.

The U.S. Department of Defense repeatedly refused any comment on the Eel's presumed location, or even that the ship was at sea, when contacted by several news agencies.

Hendricks, the BBC correspondent, corroborated the recollections of the others who saw the dolphin, and claimed to have scribbled some notes.

'I am positive that the dolphin told myself and Dr Jamison, who were the first two people to see him, about the species' ability to communicate with us in clear, understandable language by transmitting thoughts directly in a manner that would be something like what humans call ESP (extra-sensory perception).

'He said it was a routine thing for dolphins, and that if humans will step back from the edge of disaster and live in peace with the other creatures who share their planet, dolphins would enjoy speaking with us regularly.

'He was very clear about a few points, and each of us who were present this morning can repeat some of these phrases exactly because – however he did it – we all heard them.

'The dolphin did not explain how this conversation actually worked, and said any detailed discussion of that would have to wait for another time. He repeated that communication with man once was common, but was stopped because of the way humans were evolving. He listed perhaps a dozen events or practices created by man that are destroying the planet or its inhabitants, and said communication had become necessary again in order for man to understand how close we are to global catastrophe.

'That was when he gave a quick summary of dolphins' abilities to cripple mankind – within a day, he said – and we're all sure he made references to imagining the sea and sky and the entire world filled with waves of sound at levels a hundred times too strong for any human technology to withstand.

'And he definitely told us about the submarine, which he said was stopped simply as a way of letting the world's most powerful country know that it would be helpless if it chose to be belligerent – rather than taking the time to grasp this new reality.'

Dr MacDonald recalled that the dolphin asked that the United Nations form an emergency committee on global preservation, and that scientists of all nations come together to discuss how nature must be respected for the planet to survive.

All six witnesses to this morning's event repeated the dolphin's parting words exactly.

Dr MacDonald quoted the conclusion: *'The dolphin said, "I have told you many things in a short time. But it is an irony that I will leave you with a question instead of another statement. I ask mankind: Why is there such a thing as war?" '*

Gabriel, the former high-profile correspondent who apparently had some part in planning this unique gathering, has a part-time residence in the northern Scottish town of Avoch – just a few miles from Chanonry Point – where the dolphin event took place.

Gabriel offered no comment when contacted by the news agencies involved in meeting the dolphin, but did speak to Hendricks – a former colleague at the BBC – and said that she enjoyed seeing humans and dolphins interacting.

'No one was hurt, no one need be hurt, and I think you would agree that – assuming these reports about Spike are correct – history was made this morning,' Gabriel told Hendricks. 'I hope that someday future generations will look back and say this little piece of wonder at Chanonry Point was the beginning of a beautiful time.'

Gabriel told Hendricks she had 'absolutely no knowledge' of any dolphins' involvement in the American submarine incident. 'I didn't even know there was such a thing until you informed me about it,' she told him.

Gabriel apparently phoned the BBC later to repeat that she had no knowledge of anything to do with the submarine, that she intended to leave the area for a brief time to avoid being harassed, but that she would issue a statement concerning the Moray Firth dolphins to all major media outlets within the next 48 hours.

Looking back, I should have known that Spike would play a card he hadn't shown us. I know he must have done it to help to keep us as safe as possible, but the shock was beyond anything I'd ever experienced.

Jill and I kept staring at the screen, then looking at each other, and then turning back to the screen.

So much for our belief that we knew exactly what Spike would say to his hand-picked audience that morning.

We were stunned.

'Did you call Andy back?' I asked her. 'I'm assuming you had that first chat with him while I was returning the car.'

'No… and yes. I talked to him briefly, because when I dropped him off at the hotel, he told me that all six people were going to meet immediately, and that they already had pretty much decided they had no choice but to get the word out via teleconference right away. He wanted a quote from me, which made sense, because obviously I'd been part of the whole thing. So I gave Andy that soft quote, and told him to add that we talked a second time, and that I was going out of town and so forth. You can see that he ran it just as I said it.

'I really hadn't decided what to say in any kind of statement, but I thought mentioning forty-eight hours would give us some time to think it through, and maybe hear from Spike. And I felt that what I said would calm people down around the whole Moray Firth area, and give a proper version of our participation. I didn't want to do anything else without talking to you – or Spike.'

As for my reaction, well, I'm not sure exactly what I was thinking after such a staggering surprise.

Three reporters and three scientists each had listened to a dolphin speak for half an hour. That in itself was spectacular news, but what had followed about the US submarine simply left me numb.

'You know,' Jill said, 'we should have guessed the dolphins would do something to prove the existence and power of their ultrasound capacity, so that their plea to the world was not just dismissed like a Greenpeace press release. Do you think Spike would have told us about the submarine if we'd asked him directly about their plans?'

'Nope,' I replied.

'Why not?'

'C'mon, Jilly. You were in the media. Now you're going to be hunted by the media, and this is just the start. And you're innocent – at least on the submarine thing. Spike knew the sky would fall down on us. He was trying to make it as gentle as possible.

'Remember his words about us perhaps being in some danger? That whole business seemed a bit overly dramatic at the time, but he was absolutely, spot-on accurate. So he was making sure we had total and truthful deniability on the whole submarine issue. And I'm *very* glad he did.'

Jill took a deep breath before saying anything more.

'Hoo, boy,' she said. 'When I gave Andy that quote, I wasn't really planning to leave Avoch. I was just tossing it out there to slow things down for a couple of days. I figured that the fascination about dolphins actually communicating with humans would be the big story. I wasn't expecting such a direct threat, and aimed at the United States, to boot.'

'But now you're going to leave,' I told her firmly.

'I am?'

'Yes, you are. In fact, *we* are. Spike lined this all out for me in one of those little conversations where he just kind of pops into my mind and I know he's there. No, he didn't tell me about the submarine, but he mentioned that the media would come after everyone involved, and that we could expect to hear from the government, too.'

'The government?' Jill said. 'You mean the British government?'

'Sure, but now from what we just read, they're also likely to have a couple of American admirals with them. Not to mention some serious men with dark suits and sunglasses. This is the kind of thing that makes military people want to bomb somebody, just for the heck of it. That's how they think – and I suppose that's why Spike asked everyone why there is such a thing as war.

'If I'm being cynical, I would say that it's to keep some of these people in jobs, and these are the very ones who'll be coming to see us pretty soon. They'll talk to all the people who heard Spike this morning right away, but the trail will lead back to you in a heartbeat.

'You've got to go, girl. You think the United States of America will sit back and have a laugh about a nuclear submarine being held hostage for eight hours?'

I had been keeping a small secret from Jill. Originally I had thought it to be fairly harmless, but now that Spike had told all of mankind to shape up or face the consequences, things had escalated rather spectacularly.

'Spike asked me to have plane tickets for two in my pocket by Thursday night,' I told her. 'He thinks, and I agree, that perhaps in a month or so the heat mostly will be off us – and on to the people who run world governments and on other decision-makers. The dolphins apparently have a few more things planned if needed, just to keep everything in the forefront of the news, and to keep the pressure on people who matter.

'Sweetie, the dolphins are awfully smart, and they've been planning this for more than a decade. I wanted to tell you about the tickets, but Spike made me promise not to say anything until we had to face the aftermath.

'Anyhow, we're prepared, and better than you might think.'

Jill appeared a bit glassy-eyed, as though she'd taken a punch to the jaw and needed a minute for the cobwebs to clear. But I knew her pretty well. I didn't think it would take long, and it didn't.

'Was it just a week or so ago that I phoned you in America and begged you to come to Scotland?' she asked. 'Seemed like I was a pretty cool chick there for a while, and that I was really in control of things. No wonder I got shot in Bosnia. I can't quite spot the really big clues. Maybe I'd better save my cute tartan dress.'

At least she was smiling again.

'Not to worry,' I replied. 'You'll be back in control very shortly. That's your job in this relationship.'

'Thank you.'

I wanted to keep Jill relaxed. Yet at the same time there was a sense of urgency, so I told her, 'Of course you'll always make your own decisions. And some of mine, too, if you'd like. But not right this minute, and not tonight in Avoch, dear. What you need to do now is to go and buy a wig, and get some sunglasses. Then we'll start watching all the news reports. Trust Spike on this. Just as he told us, the world won't ever be the same.'

'Then tell me now,' she said. 'Will it be better or worse?'

'I'd say thumbs up. Spike's optimistic, and because he knows more than anyone, I suppose I'm a believer. I'm also a natural optimist. But there's going to be considerable chaos in the meantime.'

Jill grinned and said, 'Well, good. You came to Scotland, we had great apple pie, we talked to a dolphin and we've set the world on fire. What a nice time, except that now I can't even stay in my own house.'

'That shouldn't be a problem,' I told her.

164

'No?'

There was so much emotion in the air that I had to stop for a minute and give her a hug. Despite the cute little exchanges, we were both still a little bit shaky.

'What about the Wild West?' I suggested at last. 'Do you fancy sitting it out in the Arizona mountains while the world gets on with all the yelling and arguing?'

'Sure, why not?' she replied. 'You crossed the Atlantic for me. I can go the other way. When are we out of here?'

'Tonight.'

'Oh, good. I forgot to pick up anything for supper, anyway.'

'Looks like we get a pizza,' I said, as cheerfully as possible.

Epilogue

Flagstaff, Arizona

October

Spike certainly was right about causing a fuss.

In my log home, surrounded by forest, Jill leafed through a copy of Time magazine – the issue which pictured two leaping dolphins on the cover – and tossed it on to the coffee table. It landed next to the mid-September issue of Newsweek, which had split the front into facing pictures of Spike and the president of the United States.

Jill slid open the screen door to my back porch and came out to sit under the towering Ponderosa pines, which cover the rear side of my house. Our chairs were facing the first hole of Aspen Hills Golf Club, about 180 yards from the tee box on the right side of the fairway, which is roughly where most weekend golfers will knock their very first shot of the day. Fortunately the trees are so thick that they protect the house from direct hits.

'What are you thinking?' she asked.

'That you can really smell the pine today,' I replied.

'Seriously?'

'Sure.'

'Okay, let me start again,' Jill said, pulling over one of the deck chairs. 'What are you thinking about the dolphins?'

'Hmmm…'

Jill tried once more. 'Come on, what do you think is happening?'

'Oh, I think they're swimming and playing and eating fish by the truckload. You know, the way dolphins do.'

'And what else?' she asked, staring at the forest.

That was the big question, and of course we'd been wondering about it almost non-stop in the weeks since we traded in the Moray coast for pine-covered northern Arizona. There had been plenty of buzzing all over the world since our fateful morning at Chanonry Point. In fact, trying to follow the fallout online, or watching TV and so forth, had become pretty darn wearisome.

Initially, the US Navy did exactly what we'd expected. It denied that anything unusual had occurred on the USS Eel. It claimed that the submarine was on routine patrol at points undisclosed with no problems whatsoever.

Military thinkers are a cinch to react with short-term, save-the-moment solutions, so a flat denial was totally predictable – but also ridiculous, because no massive deception like this one could last more than a few days. And it didn't.

For one thing, the Navy would have had to involve all or most of the Eel's crew, the majority of whom had wives or families at home who were hearing hundreds of various news reports and besieging the Department of Defense with urgent, panicky inquiries.

Anyone with an ounce of sense would have realised immediately that denial of the entire incident had no chance to hold up for more than a few days – let alone forever. The whole attempt was crazy.

So then, a few slightly brighter spin doctors stepped on to the scene, and the US government announced – in its particularly aggravating manner – that yes, the USS Eel had experienced an 'undisclosed' power drop during a normal mission, that the problem had been corrected very quickly, and that the ship and all hands were back on patrol, defending the free world as usual.

In this era of CNN, the internet and endless probing reporters, however, that wasn't nearly good enough, and the Navy was subjected to a barrage of questions that put its bosses under considerable political pressure.

So finally a 'follow-up advisory' was issued, which noted that although the ship detected neither hostile action in the area nor any 'paranormal' conditions, it had been stuck without propulsion or any live communications for eight hours on September 8.

Very significantly, this was an admission that the statement Spike had made to six witnesses – which a Navy spokesman called 'not credible' at a subsequent press conference – was far more than credible.

It was undeniable fact.

Crucially, Spike had told the media at Chanonry about the submarine incident while it was in progress, and had stated the exact time that the submarine would be freed – which reporters dutifully pointed out. So at that point the Navy, and the entire US government, stopped responding to any questions about the mysterious Eel.

Among the admirals' difficulties was the fact that nothing short of a wholesale conspiracy could hide the fact that no military installation had received any kind of communication from the Eel during those eight missing hours. They had nothing to show, and nothing to say.

What Jill and I knew, because Spike had told me just before we left Scotland, was that the Navy would get another surprise when they examined the ship, because it would not show even the tiniest trace of damage.

We had no more information than that, but Jill and I both guessed that the dolphins had done something to the water *around* the vessel rather than to the submarine itself – had wrapped it in a cocoon of sound, or something like that.

The lack of visible damage would no doubt tempt the Navy to go for another round of denials. But to us it meant that the dolphins had yet another unusual ability that nobody understood – and we imagined that dozens or even hundreds of dolphins must have participated. In other words, Spike's statement that the entire species had taken up this decision to confront mankind was turning from hearsay into something approaching absolute indisputable truth.

Plenty of interesting things were going on elsewhere around the globe, as well. Dolphins turned up in Australia, South America and on both coasts of the United States to initiate short but friendly 'conversations' with humans. If these meetings once might have been dismissed as the figment of someone's imagination, they now had become simply more items to toss on to a growing stack of positive evidence.

Needless to say, all participants from what the media had dubbed 'The Chanonry Encounter' appeared frequently on chat shows, in newspaper interviews and so on.

News can be slowed in some countries but never entirely stopped. Word of the dolphin communication found its way into each nook and cranny of every nation. In most of the world, you couldn't pick up a paper, read a magazine or listen to a political debate without coming across serious discussion of the 'dolphin issue.'

Scientists, being scientists, squabbled and disagreed. But those who proposed some explanation other than the obvious were losing ground by the hour. In fact, one panel of marine and environmental experts convened by the United Nations had already suggested that experiments once proposed by John Lilly several decades earlier be re-instituted by a consortium of nations, as soon as possible. These particular experiments were to involve establishing communication with dolphins by creating computer programmes that could translate the animals' clicks and whistles into audible, recognisable language.

Jill and I laughed at that, and decided the UN would probably be better off just asking the dolphins how to proceed. The UN group was still meeting almost daily, and promised more initiatives to capitalise on what three of its spokesmen told an international press conference was an 'undeniably historic opportunity.'

In the Arizona mountains, Jill and I were beginning to believe that perhaps the dolphins had picked almost the perfect strategy for their confrontation with mankind. We had gone from being nervous about the submarine incident to being greatly heartened by it, and interpreted the USS Eel event as stage one of a plan to do only what was needed to gain and hold human attention. We believed that, if necessary, the dolphins intended to 'stair-step' their way into forcing mankind to reverse its ridiculous course. We believed that the dolphins had already mapped out a series of possible escalations, and that these would be used as needed in the task of changing mankind's direction and thus saving the planet.

First they were seeking to establish effective communication, which by now almost no one was denying. They no doubt hoped that this would quickly establish that they had powers and abilities which humans couldn't understand, or resist. If it became clear that the human race truly had gone mad and had set itself on an irreversible path toward destruction, then the dolphins held out the option of increasing the pressure with slightly more drastic measures – which we shuddered even to contemplate.

We knew just how difficult it was for these gentle creatures to abandon millions of years of living 'the natural way' for such a sad, but pivotal, intervention. What they'd done so far wouldn't scar their souls, but what if man forced them to go further?

Since Spike had told me there would be no sign of damage to the Eel, Jill had posed a very reasonable question:

'If dolphins can "imprint" human minds as easily as Spike did with us, and presumably do it without the recipient even knowing what's happened – why not just have a dolphin swim up the Potomac River to Washington and "convince" the President of the United States that the country needed massive shifts in thinking and policy? If the US moved dramatically in a different direction, the rest of the world would follow so much more quickly.'

We kept on talking about this, and our best guess was that the dolphins perhaps believed that 're-programming' a single individual wouldn't be enough. In time there would be new presidents, and other governments with weapons and a lack of sensible policy – and so it would go on. We decided that the dolphins must believe they had to reach mankind as a whole, and anything short of that might turn out to be only a temporary reprieve.

One other issue required some thought. Spike had suggested that Jill and I would always be safer – in case of government pursuit or something scary like that – if we were close to open sea, and thus closer to dolphins who might help us in an emergency. But we knew only too well that if people from some shadowy agency truly meant to harm us, they eventually would succeed – and so we agreed to carry on our normal lives in whatever surroundings we chose. We were not going to let a fear of bullies dictate our behaviour.

In the meantime, routine craziness around the world continued to be, yes, crazy. But there was one major change – dolphins were now a central theme for discussion.

Religious leaders, legitimate and otherwise, claimed all sorts of divine inspiration involving the dolphin phenomenon – some suggesting that they'd talked to dolphins, or God, or both, in private conversations.

Not surprisingly, dolphin parks and oceanariums were mobbed. Suddenly, everyone wanted to get close to some dolphins. No doubt the animals themselves were amused at their increasing popularity. At some high-profile dolphin shows, trainers would occasionally ask the audience for a moment of silence to wish the Cetaceans good luck in their effort to improve the planet for everyone.

It was all great theatre, as I'm sure Spike and his friends must have known it would be.

Sometimes we imagined him at sunset off the Moray coast – where scores of boats and helicopters had become a bit of a nuisance – chuckling away at the nuttiness of humans in general.

But we kept our optimism guarded. For instance, it took no imagination at all to picture a group of American military leaders meeting in an underground room to draw up several 'alternative options' that would be nothing more than shorthand for an all-out assault to rid the sea of dolphins – violently and quickly.

Such a course of action made no sense and would be condemned by millions, but America had acted idiotically before under the guise of 'national security', and we expected that the president had been briefed on at least a dozen military options to deal with what the generals and admirals would eloquently describe as a threat to the entire free world.

Politicians who go along with these 'shock-and-awe' assaults are financed almost entirely by big business – which includes plenty of people who have huge sums of money tied up in offshore oil and other interests that, at the very least, would have to be re-engineered if the dolphins' world vision became reality.

A safer and better world would drain plenty of powerful bank accounts, and since money has dictated insane policy decisions too many times to count, there was still cause for considerable anxiety.

But we consoled ourselves with the knowledge that for a decade and more, the most intelligent creatures on the planet had thought about this scenario from start to finish. The dolphins were infinitely smarter, incredibly better informed and, although the world's military hawks might want to deny it, possessed 'weaponry' which man had never seen or imagined.

We thought that Spike's chances of succeeding were very good, indeed, but how could anyone be sure if greed or self-interest or just plain stupidity might entice someone to create a bloodbath before conceding that the world would have to be saved, or even managed, by another species?

While we were hanging around in our pine-covered retreat, waiting to see how things developed, we tried hard not to worry all day and night about the dolphins and the world's new dilemma – or 'opportunity,' as we liked to think of it.

When we'd been back in Scotland, Jill had mentioned briefly that she'd taken up golf. October is a gorgeous month in the Arizona mountains, so we got out to play a few times. When Jill attacked the game with fervour, I shouldn't have been surprised. However, she hit enough trees to be designated a hazard to the environment all by herself.

And since the only thing Tiger Woods and I have in common is wearing the same brand of golf glove, Jill and I often teed off together, and then met again only at the green – after taking various scenic routes and scaring dozens of squirrels. We were fairly pitiful golfers, but it was fun, the air is clean and fresh at 7,000 feet, and we got some exercise tramping around in the woods after errant golf balls. And for a few hours, it occasionally took our minds off the massive issue we had helped to create.

Then another kind of news came our way.

Jill had given my e-mail address and phone number to the media people and scientists whom she felt that she could trust, and asked that we get word when anybody heard something worthwhile.

One morning we got a startling call from Barbara Williamson, who was ringing not with any hot breaking news, but because she'd been approached as an intermediary. A giant publishing house wanted to offer Jill a seven-figure advance to write a book about the entire dolphin adventure.

We talked it over that night, and decided that a book project wouldn't do the dolphins any harm at all, and perhaps Jill could continue to help their cause with a best-seller in every shop window.

'If they'll let us do it together, I'll take it,' she announced over tea the next morning. 'We can keep a little of the money to live on, and use most of it to start a foundation or some sort of fund. I'll bet Spike would have some really great ideas about how to get programmes going to help educate people about dolphins and whales. Hey, what if our next generation of schoolkids could learn about dolphins by actually talking to them?'

I went quiet for a bit, and my mind wandered all over the place, thinking through the events of the past few weeks. Relaxing on the back porch was an ideal place to still the mind, and so once again, that's where we happened to be.

Jill asked, 'Did I lose you there?'

'No, not at all,' I replied. 'Really, I was just thinking about Spike... everything that's happened... and the possibilities. Sorry.'

'That's okay,' Jill said. 'You know, I'm still scared for the dolphins. And for everyone, really. We've helped start something that isn't going to stop. Maybe it will open the door to an amazing new world, but...'

'I know,' I said, taking her hand. 'Is mankind brave enough to accept it?'

AUTHOR'S NOTE

This story is a work of fiction. A remarkably large share of it, however, is based on fact.

Several of the unique and amazing abilities possessed by dolphins have been documented numerous times, even though scientists only began serious study of the species *Cetacea* barely more than a half-century ago.

Anyone who has swum with dolphins, or has been anywhere near them, can testify to what researchers confirm. It seems that these creatures are able to 'read' us internally with a type of ultra-sound that is only now becoming common in modern medicine. The same is true of dolphins' echolocation capabilities and their power to stun fish – with a 'weapon' that countless observers have reported is never used for any other purpose, not even self-defence.

But can dolphins 'speak' to humans?

One character in this novel is based on a real-life researcher who has worked closely with dolphins for most of his life, and this is how he describes the possibility: 'It wouldn't be a very long leap.'

All reports concerning the stranded whale who visited London in 2006 were taken directly from newspaper accounts, and the quoted material from Science Daily is accurate.

But this book is still fiction, as are most of the characters. Despite what so many people assume, I really don't know anyone called Jill Gabriel – who is based loosely on several outstanding female journalists whose work I've admired.

Likewise, I've invented the pleasant young Daisy, the magazine editor Bo Tremaine and many other important figures in the book – including the enjoyable Samantha and the Vascuso brothers, though I admit to knowing some people who seem a lot *like* that fun family.

There is no submarine called the USS Eel, although there might have been. The United States Navy was building a Balao class sub (SS-354) during World War II, but construction was cancelled in October of 1944 and there hasn't been another ship of that name until we 'created' our very own.

On the other hand, not only is there a flourishing colony of Atlantic bottlenose dolphins in and around the Moray Firth in northern Scotland, but one of them actually is called Spike by researchers from the University of Aberdeen field station. The local dolphins are identified by marks on their bodies and by various colour shadings, and are then 'named' for future spotting purposes.

And about 7,000 miles away, yes, that amazing scene involving the young girls at the dolphin petting pool in California happened as described. I witnessed it exactly as you read it in the book.

Most of the locations in the United States, England and Scotland have been described as accurately as possible.

There definitely is terrific apple pie at a little café in Auchterarder. Tales of the Seer and his fate at Chanonry Point could be true – the locals insist on it – and places like Inverness, Avoch and Fortrose are right where you'll find them in this narrative. So are Houston and Miami, and they're both as mind-numbingly hot and humid as I've claimed in the story.

Stephen – yes, that's me – is definitely a fan of Arsenal Football Club in north London, and you can find some very good company at The Twelve Pins pub on

Seven Sisters Road – where I meet with the fictional Dr Ian Edwards. By the way, I did have such an interview, but the name of the real-life researcher has been changed, and it took place in a Scottish village. The dialogue from our actual discussion was very close to what you find in the chat with Dr Edwards.

Although you will find this book correctly classified as fiction, I'd like you to think of it as a story of reasonable logic mixed with hope. It does include a large amount of factual information – which can be proven with any simple search.

But then there is a third part, the real soul of the book, which requires, well...

That you decide for yourself.

Steve Cameron
Edinburgh
2013

ABOUT THE AUTHOR

Steve Cameron is an American journalist who has written 14 books, in addition to working for newspapers and magazines in the United States, Great Britain and Qatar.

Born and raised in San Francisco, the grandson of well-known Scottish engineer Francis Gordon -- who led design of the original Aswan Dam in Egypt -- Steve began his writing and communications career in the Midwestern US. He eventually became an author, radio talk-show host and international conference moderator.

An American citizen with permanent UK residency, Cameron currently spends his time in northern California, Kansas City and the Moray Coast of Scotland.

Follow Steve on Twitter at @stevecameron100

Other titles from Augur Press

Now Is Where We Are:
Poems from the Priory Hospital
by Hilary Lissenden

ISBN 978-0-9558936-7-4   £6.99

"That there is a link between psychiatric illness and creativity seems widely accepted, although not completely understood. The 'black dog' of clinical depression has kept me intermittent company since my early teens, and I have often written prolifically while recovering from periods of depressive illness."

Once read, these poems will always be your companions. By turns they move and delight with their beauty, wit and depth of fellow-feeling. These are the real thing.

Dr Iain McGilchrist
Consultant Psychiatrist, The Priory Hospital
Former Fellow in English Literature, Oxford University

Order from your local bookshop, amazon.co.uk or the Augur Press website at www.augurpress.com

The Voice Within
by Catherine Turvey

ISBN 978-0-9558936-3-6   £5.99

"Creative writing is a wonderful way to express and deal with all sorts of emotions and feelings related to the real world we live in, and everyday life. I was inspired to put all my work together in a book, when family and friends requested copies of my work to keep or to show others. I felt that if my few words could help people in any way by bringing comfort, hope, or encouragement, then why not bring it together for all those who would be interested?"

These poems are the work of a gifted child.

Order from your local bookshop, amazon.co.uk or the Augur Press website at www.augurpress.com

Beyond the Veil

ISBN 0-9549551-4-5 £8.99

Fay

ISBN 0-9549551-3-7 £8.99

Emily

ISBN 978-0-9549551-8-2 £8.99

a trilogy by Mirabelle Maslin

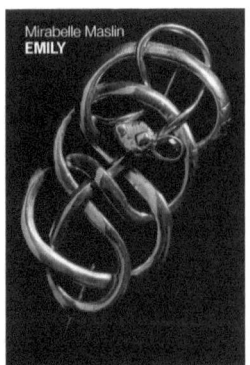

Spiral patterns, a strange tape of music from Russia, a 'blank' book and an oddly shaped walking stick ...

Fay suffers from a mysterious illness. In her vulnerable state, she is affected by something more than intuition ...

Emily meets Barnaby. Sensing that they have been drawn together for a common purpose, they discover that each carries a crucial part of an unfinished puzzle from years past ...

Order from your local bookshop, amazon.co.uk or the Augur Press website at www.augurpress.com

For all other titles from Augur Press
please visit

www.augurpress.com